Julie's Tree

Julie's Tree
by Mary Calhoun

HARPER & ROW, PUBLISHERS
New York
Cambridge, Philadelphia, San Francisco, Washington
London, Mexico City, São Paulo, Singapore, Sydney

Library of Congress Cataloging-in-Publication Data
Calhoun, Mary.
   Julie's tree.

   Summary: After the death of her mother, Julie leaves
her grandmother's home to join her father in a new town
where she must adjust to new friends and tries to save a
tree threatened by a new parking lot.
   [1. Moving, Household—Fiction.   2. Single-parent
family—Fiction.   3. Schools—Fiction.   4. Trees—
Fiction]   I. Title.
PZ7.C1278Ju   1988   [Fic]   87-45857
ISBN 0-06-020995-X
ISBN 0-06-020996-8 (lib. bdg.)

To Amy, Cher and Rete, keepers of the tree

Julie's Tree

1

The real adventure, the good times and the troubles, began when Julie found the tree.

At the school-bus stop, getting off with the others, she said, "Good-bye," but nobody seemed to hear her. No one said, "Come on, Julie." Maybe one time the girls had said it, when she was watching a dragon-shaped cloud. She'd noticed one girl looking at her and whispering, "She's too stuck-up."

If her grandmother, Frannie, could see her trailing along like a ghost behind the other kids, she'd insist on Julie coming home. She could just hear Gram's warm husky voice, "Honey, you come right back here, where you've got friends."

Actually, having a lot of friends had never seemed

important. At home she had one good friend, Amy, and some buddies in swim class. They were all she'd needed until this move and the big question: Will Julie Adjust?

Walking by herself she'd feel less alone than following those kids. Julie went back to Fourth Street to go home a new way, and halfway down the hill she discovered a wilderness in the midst of all the buildings of town. Except for a small parking area nicked out of the corner, it was half a block both ways of bushes and hollows and high grass. An overgrown path cut across, so Julie took this shortcut.

And there, back by the alley, was the tree.

She'd never seen a tree so tall and so bushy at the top. It was so thick with leaves it took up as much space as a three-story house. What's more, the way the lower branches were spaced, it looked like it could be the best climbing tree yet!

Julie rated trees by how good they would be to climb. Back home her best tree was the cherry tree in Frannie's side yard, although now that she was ten it was almost too little to climb. This summer she'd barely wedged into the branches to eat cherries the fairies had pecked.

Not that she ever mentioned the fairies. Nobody in fourth grade last year had believed in fairies. Some kids believed in Bigfoot or the Swamp Monster. Nobody believed in fairies.

Julie stood under the tree to study the route up. Once she got into the first crotch, she could step on the long bough to the right, swing around the trunk to one that elbowed at the back, then reach up for— Yes, there was a regular winding staircase to the top of the tree!

The only trouble was, the first crotch was too high for her to get into it. She spread her arms on the trunk to try to knee her way up, but this was a huge old hero of a tree. Its trunk was too wide for her to get a grip. She needed a booster step.

Julie looked around. Toward the front of the vacant land were the rubbly remains of a house's foundation—some bricks—nothing big enough. A high tangled hedge walled the lot off from a house next door. Julie snooped along the hedge back toward the tree, until she found a big boulder. If she could get it over to the foot of the tree . . .

Just as she reached for the rock, something made her look up at the hedge. A twinkle of leaves—she thought she saw eyes looking through the leaves at her.

Julie froze, staring at the eyes. They didn't move. The bushes were too much of a thicket to see the shape of a body beyond them. After a long stillness Julie decided it was a trick of the light between the small leaves.

Using a stick, she pried the boulder out of the

ground, then got behind it and heaved. The stone rolled easily, like magic, as if the tree were drawing it.

Julie settled the big rock between roots to steady it, mounted, and the height was just enough. Grasping the trunk where it divided, she pulled herself up into the crotch.

To climb a tree for the first time meant the adventure of exploring it. Julie held on to the trunk while she walked up the right-hand branching, then stepped out on the long level bough. It thrust up another small branch just right for an armhold, so Julie tried the bough first. And a fine place it was to sit, too, swinging her legs in the air, arm around the small branch. She bounced, and the bough dipped a little.

At the motion there was a skirmish higher among the leaves. Julie saw a squirrel run out along a limb and leap to a tree in the back yard next door. There the squirrel set up a long chatter of scolding at the invader.

"I'm sorry, Squirrel," Julie called. "I didn't know somebody else was in the tree."

What kind of tree was it? The bark was ridged, creasing into her legs, not smooth like sycamore bark. Oval leaves with ragged edges—not a maple—and up there a September-dry berry, purple . . . Of course! It must be a mulberry tree. In her aunt's back yard there had been a mulberry tree, and once when she was little, Dad had put her up on a branch to reach for the sweet berries.

When she stood on the bough, the squirrel gave another chatter of alarm. Julie edged back to the trunk and climbed. It was a matter of testing which were the right steps of the circular staircase. Not there, that was a dead end. Squeeze between those branches . . . don't use that one, not strong enough. (Julie had too much respect for a tree to fall out of one or break branches.) Here was another crotch, a stair landing to rest on.

And a hollow in the tree, right at eye level. Down in the dark hollow she spied a nest of leaves, probably the squirrel's nest. Were there young ones? Putting her cheek against the rough bark, Julie listened but heard only the distant fussing of the squirrel.

A late-afternoon breeze had come up. The leaves whispered, and the upper part of the tree swayed. Julie swayed with it.

Once she'd heard a grown-up talk about climbing on a tree, but she knew better. You don't climb *on* a tree; you climb *in* it.

Exploring upward, at last at the top of the staircase, she was higher than she'd ever been in a tree before. In the topmost branches that would support her, she looked out to see what she could see from there.

Back beyond the school-bus stop, two church spires

lifted above the trees and shone in sunlight. She could see the roofs of buildings down along Main Street and, closer, the top of a brick building just across the street. A rhythm sounded softly from it, *clack-clack-ti-clack-clack*, maybe some kind of factory. She looked for the house Dad had rented, but there was too much leafiness between.

Arm around a branch, Julie gave a sigh of satisfaction. She was part of the treetop-ness, the rooftop-ness of the town.

Now she could look over the hedge of the house next door. It seemed a very private place, nestled between the hedge and a building like a high brick wall. Yet from the tree she could see into an upper window under the peaked roof. By the alley was a shed and the tree the squirrel had jumped to, a pear tree, she thought. Julie looked down into the back garden, reds and sunset yellows, zinnias and marigolds.

Then a rusty bush moved and became a woman, a small woman crouching about, doing things to the earth. A moment before, Julie wouldn't have believed there was a human there. So small—an elf woman?

Was it her eyes that had looked through the hedge? Silently watching, not moving— What kind of woman would do that?

A calico cat appeared from under a bush and leaned against the woman. She touched it, and then, as if she sensed Julie's gaze, the woman looked up at the mulberry tree. White hair wisped from under the brown cap on her head. No expression showed on the weathered face, but Julie knew the woman had seen her.

And there, a man came out of the factory to a car in the parking area. *Don't look up,* Julie willed. Usually grown-ups didn't. She melted against the branches: *I'm part of the tree.* He didn't see her. He got into the car and drove off.

Julie let out her breath and uncramped her legs. Maybe the tree, back here by the alley, was far enough away from both streets that nobody would notice her. She wanted this to be a wild private place. There wasn't a single climbing tree at the house Dad had rented.

When she let herself down from branch to step-branch, the woman in the garden didn't look up again. Good. The woman wasn't going to pay any attention to her.

Julie followed the path out to Jefferson Street and ran. She'd lost track of time in the tree. Dad might be home and wondering where she was. She turned up the walk of the house Dad— Stop that! she told herself. It wasn't just "the house Dad had rented." It was her home now.

It was a rather tall but narrow brick house in the middle of two others just like it. They were built so close together she could hear the TV going in the house next door. At least there was a back yard that went downhill to the alley, but the one tree in it was an ancient walnut with branches starting too high to climb.

Unlocking the front door, she called, "Hello?" No answer. The clock showed five fifteen, so he wouldn't be there for a while yet. Julie went upstairs to her room.

That was the one thing she liked about this house. It was narrow and dark, but it had lots of stairs, and Julie liked to go up flights of stairs. From the back yard, steps led up to the high porch off the kitchen. There were stairs down to the basement, stairs up to the second floor, and then best of all, two steps up from the hallway to her little bedroom in the gable.

She could pretend her room was the tower of her enchanted castle. From her tower room she could look out and see magical things, perhaps a ship sailing in the sky.

Julie started to read her library book, then remembered she was supposed to put potatoes in the oven to bake. No microwave oven at this house. No Frannie. No mother.

After supper she and Dad sat on the back porch in the dusk. It was peaceful, watching fireflies blink above the grass and up into the walnut tree, while Dad played something on his recorder.

"I made a friend today," Julie said.

Dad finished a musical phrase, then asked, "Care to tell me who she—or he—is?"

"Um—both." Julie smiled.

Dad looked at her in that way she liked, his eyebrows up.

"It's a tree. The very best tree yet, Dad! On the way—"

"Before I hear all the wonders, I'm curious. How can a tree be both male and female?"

"Easy. In the summer a tree is a woman, all dressed in leaves and fruit. In the winter the tree is—" She tried to think how to say it.

"Stripped to the bone!" He made a wry sound. "Like some men I know."

"Oh, Dad! No"—she thought of the clean outline of a tree—"in winter the branches are like strong bare arms."

"Julie's a poet and doesn't know it!" He played a riff of appreciation on the recorder.

"Anyway, this tree has a regular winding staircase of—"

The phone rang, and Dad went in to answer it. When he came back, his face was polite, and she knew before he said it, "It's your grandmother."

Frannie must really miss her, calling every few days. "I miss you, too," she told her grandmother, "but you sound so close, it's like you're here. How are things at the shop?"

"Sweetie, that's why I'm calling," Frannie said.

"This weekend I'm going to market in St. Louis, so tell me, what special things do you want?"

"Oh, Gram— You pick."

Her grandmother owned Frannie's Flair, a dress shop that featured the latest clothing and accessories for girls and young women. Julie knew she was a disappointment to Gram, not caring much about clothes.

She said, "See if there's any jeans with jazzy knee patches and seaters."

Gram laughed, asking once again, "Have you made any friends?"

"Yes." A tree. She couldn't tell her that. To Frannie, friends were people and maybe some dogs. Frannie just didn't understand how hard it was, because she had always had friends.

"Uh, there's this girl, Sandy. She's got the funniest laugh. She goes *e-yuck, e-yuck, yuck.*" Julie scraped the back of her throat, trying to sound like a girl on the school bus, who was also in her class.

Frannie was so happy about it that Julie let the fib stand. In answer to how things were going with Dad, she said, "Fine! He's going to make teddy bear pancakes Saturday morning and then show me around where he works." So far she'd seen only the outside of the building where he wrote computer software.

Frannie's voice cooled a little, as she said, "Let me talk to him before we hang up."

When her father went in to the phone, Julie sat

on the porch and watched fireflies bright in the darkness. This move had to work. She had to make it work.

After Mom had died, it was natural to stay on at Frannie's, where they'd all lived. Dad had been finishing his studies at the university, and although Mom had had a good job as a secretary for an insurance agency, they couldn't afford a house of their own. But when Dad moved to Sutterville last spring to start work at last as a computer software engineer, Frannie didn't want Julie to go.

"I've lost my daughter," Gram had said, her voice heavy. "Leave Julie with me. Peter, you can't make a home for her, a single man."

"Yes, I think I can," he'd said, "but she can stay until I get settled, anyway. I know we owe you a lot." Julie thought that embarrassed him. Frannie had loaned some money for his college tuition, too. "Of course, I'll send money for her support."

Julie kept on living with Frannie and playing with Amy and reading books in the back room of the shop.

But she could not bear to lose both parents. Even after a year it hurt to touch the thought of Mom— Betsy Bennett—gone. Not Dad, too.

She told Frannie, "I know I'll miss you. You— the shop—this is home. But I need to be with Dad."

"Oh, honey, I worry you'd be alone so much!"

In August Dad phoned to set the date for Julie's

13

move. After the phone call Julie remembered how she'd leaned against her grandmother's side, while they both cried a little.

"Gram, I won't stay by myself all the time," she had said. "I'll make friends there, and I'll be just fine. Gram, I promise!"

Frannie had sighed. "Oh, sweetie, all right. Try it until Christmas, and then we'll see."

Julie wondered if Frannie could make Dad see, if it wasn't working out. What if they decided it wasn't working out? Julie loved her grandmother, but she wanted to live here. She shivered, feeling the cool of the September evening. It was up to her to make a good life in a different school with new friends.

The next afternoon on the school bus she tried to make friends again. Sandy was sitting behind her and going *e-yuck, e-yuck* to another girl. Turning around, Julie said, "I like your laugh."

"What laugh?" Sandy stared at her and kept on staring until Julie felt her cheeks get hot.

She couldn't think of anything to say. She felt so clumsy with this girl just looking at her, obviously not wanting to be friends. Julie faced front. Behind her the girls whispered.

As soon as she could get off the bus, she ran to the tree.

2

Julie sat on the long bough and kicked her heels at the air. It wasn't fair. She tried to make friends. It wasn't her fault Dad had moved to another town. She couldn't help it that Mom had been hit by a car when she ran across the street against traffic.

The bough stopped bouncing, as Julie felt the same old pain, the empty place. She knew she had to go on with a new life. Frannie had talked to her about it; so had the school counselor. Dad had said, "Try not to paint your memories of your mother with unhappiness." In a way, Amy had helped most of all, just being there, a faithful friend.

She missed Amy. The first two weeks she was here they'd talked four times on the phone. They'd written to each other, but Amy's reply had said, "I'm no good at letter-writing."

Okay, she had a new life now.

Julie leaned against the arm-hold branch and looked up through the boughs. Today she should name the tree. Mulberry had a pretty sound to it, but the name didn't mean anything special about this particular mulberry tree. Maybe she'd get an idea while she climbed. Sitting on the bough, she felt as if she were still on the front porch of the tree.

As she swung around to the branch that elbowed a right angle, she noticed a few dried berries hanging from a twig the birds had missed. So . . . if the low bough was the porch—the porch swing!—then this part could be the kitchen. Actually, the whole tree had been a kitchen or dining room for birds and squirrels earlier this summer.

And the crotch that she'd thought of as a stair landing, maybe it was the living room, for she could lean her back against a branch, just like sitting in a chair. There was the hollow, Squirrel's bedroom; and in those top branches was her lookout, a tower room. One of the out-reaching boughs had been Squirrel's runway to fly to the pear tree; and up on another limb she noticed for the first time a bird's nest.

The tree was like a house full of rooms. Or apartments. When you thought of who all lived there, who hopped on or climbed on the branches . . . the strong arms of the tree . . . of course! The name of the tree was the Armstrong Apartments.

You silly. Julie smiled at herself. But she loved the idea, anyway. That was the tree's name.

It wasn't until she was nearly home that she remembered the old lady next door. She'd forgotten to check whether the elf lady was watching her.

That night she told Dad about naming the tree, and he said, "I'll have to meet this tree. I wonder if I could still—"

Julie guessed by the dreamy look in his eyes what he was thinking. He'd been a tree-climber, too, when he was a boy. She twitched her toes under the kitchen table, not sure she wanted him climbing in the tree. Much as she loved Dad, it was her private place.

However, the next day it rained, and it kept on raining Saturday, while Dad made pancakes shaped like teddy bears—"there's one short leg, there's the other"—and they toured the computer offices. In the afternoon she washed windows on the inside—"It doesn't *have* to be such a dark house." That night they watched a favorite television program, took turns reading aloud from a folktale book; and then Julie went up to her room to read some more.

As she mounted the last two steps to her room, she thought, I knew it! I knew it would be this good to be with Dad again!

When she had arrived at the end of the summer,

they'd been careful with each other, after living apart since spring. But Dad had seemed so glad to have her that he'd come out of his usual quietness. And he hadn't criticized her. Sometimes Mom had wailed that "Peter is as quiet as a tomb, except when he's criticizing," and that he lived only for his work. That was okay. Julie liked quietness, too.

After a few days of being extra jolly together, she and Dad had settled into their happy routine. While he jogged in the early mornings, she got breakfast ready—English muffins and cereal one morning, bagels and cream cheese the next. While they ate, he read the newspaper and she did homework, because part of the agreement was to keep her grades up. In the evenings they talked or went for walks or read aloud, and then they each went about their own business.

Julie undressed and got into bed. It *was* quiet, though, she thought, not looking at her book. Dad didn't seem to know anybody. Mom was the easygoing one, always bringing in people. She would have known how to handle Sandy. Without Mom there was no one to show her how to make friends.

In the night the rain stopped, and by Sunday afternoon Julie thought the tree would be dried out enough. The small factory was silent as she passed it, like a clock that didn't tick on Sundays. The other day she'd looked in dirty windows and had seen machines working, but she couldn't tell what they made. A sign on the building read only POTTER'S MFG.

Crossing the street, she saw the tree looked fresh washed, its leaves glistening. A few fairies flew away from the top of the tree. (When they were too far away to identify, they might as well be fairies as birds.) Today she planned to try climbing with her eyes shut, to find out if her feet and hands knew where the branches were yet. Probably, though, she would have to peek while she memorized the tree.

As Julie got nearer, she realized something was wrong. There was movement up there among the leaves and a shape lots bigger than a squirrel. A creature—could it be a tree dwarf? It wasn't. It was a boy.

Julie's chest felt squeezed, and her toes curled down in her sneakers, as she stood under the tree, trying to think what to do.

"Hi," the boy called. He peered over a branch, and water drops spattered down. "Come on up! Somebody put a rock there, so we can get up."

That was it. In putting the boulder under the tree, she had opened the way for others to climb.

She recognized the boy. His name was Ned, and once he had said good-bye to her at the bus stop; but she hadn't paid much attention to him, because he was only a fourth-grader. Now he was sitting in her "living room" and reaching his hand into Squirrel's hollow.

19

"Don't!" she cried out. "The squirrel might bite." Immediately she thought, what do I care if he gets bitten? "Were you coming down soon?"

"Nah, I just got here." He climbed farther, and Julie winced when she heard a branch creak. "Come on, it's a great tree to climb. And easy. Don't be afraid."

Julie sat on the boulder to wait until the stupid boy got done bumbling around in the tree. She saw him start out on a bough that bent with his weight.

"Stop!" she called. "Wait there for me. I'm coming up."

Julie scrambled up the staircase. "That branch you were on was about to break! You could have fallen, dummy!"

Ned smiled right through her scolding, and she saw she wasn't far wrong about him being a tree dwarf. Rather, he looked like a friendly elf, the way his ears were slightly pointed and his gray-green eyes tilted.

"You sure can climb a tree! You been in this one?"

"I'll show you the best way to the top," Julie answered, "if you've got to be up here. Follow me."

Her shoulders were damp from raindrops that brushed off the leaves. Then her foot slipped on wet bark.

"We shouldn't be up here," she said. "The tree is too wet for climbing."

Nevertheless, she had to pull herself up into the tower room to look out over the beautiful treetop rooftop world. Far below, the calico cat puttered in the elf lady's garden.

"But I want to get to the top, too," Ned protested. "You're in the way."

"Oh, all right. Back down a little, so I can squeeze past you."

They maneuvered around the trunk. Julie retreated to the living room, while Ned climbed into her tower room.

"Wow, this is great!" he shouted. "I've never been so high!"

"Don't make so much noise," she said. "People will notice us."

There were hardly any cars on the Sunday-quiet streets, though, and no people were walking.

"Hey, I can see my house!" Ned called in a hushed holler. "Can you see your house?"

"No."

Down here she couldn't see anything. Yes, she could. A bright eye looked over the edge of the hollow, then disappeared. Squirrel must really be scared, to not make a sound.

"Poor Squirrel, I know," Julie whispered. "We've both been invaded."

Now Ned was pumping the top branches to make them sway, scattering down raindrops. It made her sick to watch him. For herself, she knew she was careful in a tree, but— She gasped at the way the boy came down, slipping and catching himself.

"Come on," she said sharply. "Let's get down before you fall down."

"I'm not going to fall," Ned said, sliding farther than he'd meant into the crotch she'd just vacated.

Once on the ground, he stood looking back up into the tree. "That is just the greatest tree I have ever climbed," he said, his voice solemn. "Hey!" he turned to Julie. "You want to come up to my house?"

"No. I'm going home and put on some dry clothes." She headed for the path toward her street.

"Okay, see you tomorrow."

Hmph! Julie watched the boy take the path in the other direction. She walked along the sidewalk past the old lady's house and waited. Then she went back and looked. Good, he was out of sight.

She hurried to the boulder at the foot of the tree, crouched, got her arms around the rock and pulled. It didn't budge. Maybe the rain had made it settle. She got a stick and pried under it, but it didn't move an inch. Why? It had rolled easily to the tree. Julie heaved and tugged until she panted, but the boulder acted as if it had put down roots to the center of the earth.

Oh well—she gave up. Without the boulder there she couldn't get up in the tree, either. And if he really wanted to climb the tree, he could nail board steps on the trunk. Maybe he wouldn't come back.

The next morning Julie was already on the bus, trying to hide from Ned, when Sandy got on. So Julie got full benefit of what happened.

"Hi, y'all!" Sandy called out, and flashed her mouth in a big smile. She had green fangs.

"Urk!" Julie choked and laughed with the other kids.

Sandy smiled just long enough for everybody to see she had painted green points on each tooth, leaving the white glittering between. Then she snapped her mouth shut and sat down behind Julie.

"Do that again," said a boy across the aisle.

Julie turned around to watch.

"Do what?" Sandy muttered, not moving her lips away from her teeth.

"Come on!" He was in their class, Arnold, and when they were supposed to brainstorm ideas, he was the quickest.

"Gimme a nickel to make me smile." The words were guttural behind Sandy's closed lips.

Arnold poked at her ribs. "I'll give you a tickle to make you laugh!"

Sandy's mouth popped open, "Ha ha!" as she squirmed to get away from Arnold. Julie tried to see what she'd painted on her teeth. Crayon, wax?

"Hey, you kids, cut it out!" called the lady bus driver. "Back in your seats!"

Sandy gave everybody free green grins the rest of the way to school, looking like a funny monster. That was what attracted Julie to her—Sandy had imagination, and what's more, she did something about her ideas.

Like, the first week of school she'd persuaded their homeroom teacher, Mr. Armbruster, that watching a circus train unload could be a social studies project. The principal wouldn't let them use a school bus, so Sandy got her mother and other mothers to drive all twenty-six of their class down to the railway station. They were the only kids in school to get to see the circus train unload.

Afterward, Mr. Armbruster had them write papers on which job they'd like in the circus. Sandy wrote about being the tiger trainer, and Julie wrote her daydream of being a high-wire walker. But Arnold made up a long story about being the manager of a flea circus and how he charged everybody twenty-five cents extra to rent magnifying glasses, so they could really see the fleas perform.

It was too much to hope Ned would forget the tree. As she got off the bus that afternoon, he was right behind her.

"I don't have to go home yet," he said. "You want to go to the tree?"

Of course she wanted to go the tree. But not with him. However, she wasn't about to let him use the tree without her along.

Julie looked to see if Sandy or the other girls were paying attention. They weren't.

"Okay."

Julie ran ahead of him down the path and climbed to the living room at the center of the tree. Let him do what he wanted. But Ned found a branch near her to perch on.

"Don't you want to play?"

He wasn't a tree elf, Julie decided. He was more like a friendly puppy who wouldn't go away.

There was a slap of a screen door. "Ssh." Julie pointed to the little woman coming out of her house.

"Kitty-kitty!" she called in a high creak. She sped across the yard to the pear tree and gave the trunk a thump. "*Will* you come down!" On the second branch up was the white-and-orange clump of a cat. "Pshaw!" She shook the lowest branch.

"Who's she?" Ned whispered.

Julie shook her head, finger to her lips, as the woman moved to look at a late-blooming rosebush near the hedge. There was a sound, a crackle. The woman was laughing. What was so funny about the rosebush? She went to the shed, but at the door she turned and looked straight up at them. Then she went inside, leaving the cat in the tree.

"Wuh!" Ned breathed. "Did you hear that laugh?

25

And the look she gave us! Maybe she's a witch!"

"Maybe she's a fairy woman."

"Aw, come on. Fairies are tiny."

Not always, Julie told him. She'd read of fairy women who were nearly as big as people. "Anyway, I'm going to call her Griselda."

"Good," Ned agreed. "Griselda could be either a fairy or a witch."

He climbed to the tower room and began to sway the branches. Julie watched him anxiously. She could go up and hold his legs, in case he fell. But she wasn't his mother. Let him fall. Then maybe he'd stay away from the tree. Ah, but that was a mean thought. She didn't want him to get hurt. He wasn't a bad kid. Now he'd grasped the ends of two small branches and was weaving them around.

"What are you doing?" she called.

"Steering the tree. Play like this is a ship, and we're sailing, sailing— No, it's a riverboat. Hey, let's call this tree the River Queen!"

"No." Julie started up toward him. "It's already got a name."

It was natural he'd think of the river, since the Mississippi flowed past the town at the bottom of the hills. Julie leaned against the trunk just below Ned. Even from the top you couldn't see the river.

"So what's its name, then?" he asked.

Should she tell? She wanted to. "Well, this tree is like an apartment house." She explained it to him, pointing to the different branches. "It's the Armstrong Apartments, and you are in my tower room."

Ned cocked his head, thinking about that. "Okay, for you it is. For me, this is the pilot house."

And Julie thought about *that*. If he liked the tree, maybe he had as much right to imagine about it as she did. Still, it was her tree. She'd found it first.

"One day it can be the River Queen, the next—" Ned was saying, when a screech cut the air. It came from the back yard next door.

"Help! You children up there! Help me!"

3

Julie and Ned looked through the leaves to see the amazing sight of a woman in a tree. She was sprawled on her stomach across the lowest branch of the pear tree, and as they watched, she pulled herself up onto it, panting, "Drat! Drat! Drat!" On the ground lay a tipped-over stepladder. Above her the cat scrambled higher.

The woman glared up at Julie and Ned. "Come here right away! Drat!"

They climbed down, Ned coming so fast he stepped on Julie's hand—"Ow! Watch it!" Since there was no opening in the hedge, they ran back to the alley, where they found a gate in the wire fence. The woman sat on the branch, hanging on to the trunk and glowering at her rescuers. Seen up close, her face was as hard and wrinkled as a walnut, a tough-looking face for a white-haired old lady.

"Set that ladder up," she ordered, which Julie and Ned were doing. "And whichever of you laughs—"

Julie almost did, because it reminded her of an old game that ended *Whoever laughs gets a pinch, a box and a smack.* Then she gasped, as the woman tried to turn on the branch to back down the step-ladder.

"Here, let me steady you." Julie got up on the steps.

"Get out of the way! I'm all right! Just hold the ladder." She backed down, puffing.

"Don't step on your skirt," Ned advised.

"Yowl," commented the cat from an upper branch.

"Drat that cat!" The small woman stood on the ground looking up, fists on her hips. "Never climbs a tree. Can't get down."

The cat looked down, and Julie saw it had blue eyes. With its orange, brown and white fur, it was as colorful as a fairy tale cat.

"I'll get it for you," Ned volunteered.

He swarmed up the ladder and into the tree. Shinnying up the trunk to the next usable limb, he called, "Here, kitty."

The cat moaned and backed around nervously to retreat.

"What's your cat's name?" Ned asked, climbing.

"Puss. Watch what you're doing!"

"Here, Puss, Puss."

"Oh, Ned, be careful!" Julie called.

At the same time, he thrust his foot against a branch to pull himself up. There was an ominous crack, and the slender bough dangled, broken.

"If it wasn't bad enough, having a bunch of children playing next door, now they come and break my poor tree!"

Ned looked at the broken branch below him. He exclaimed, "Now what do I do? That was my stair-step down."

Julie laughed. She couldn't help it. First one creature, then another, the pear tree was snagging them all.

"What are you laughing at?" the woman snapped.

"I'm sorry," Julie apologized, still smiling, "but it's like the fairy tale about the golden goose. First one person stuck to it, then another person stuck to it and— It's like your pear tree is magic, capturing one creature after another."

The old woman looked at her queerly. "You like fairy tales and magic?"

"Yes."

"Hey, down there," Ned called. "This is no time for stories."

"Okay, now it's my turn." Julie started up the ladder. "I think I can help you," she told Ned. She was taller than he was. "See if you can reach the cat."

"Grab her by the back of the neck," the cat's mistress instructed. "She'll go limp."

Julie leaned against the trunk, standing awkwardly on the limb below the broken one, while Ned pulled up farther toward Puss. A pear tree wasn't nearly as easy to climb as the mulberry tree, even though the boughs angled closer together.

The cat darted a paw to scratch, then, "Got her!" Ned exclaimed. Gripping the cat by the back of its neck, he pulled it against his chest. "Puss, Puss, good Puss—yeah." He eased down, holding the trunk with his other arm.

When he was above her, Julie reached to steady his ankles. "Try to step down on my shoulders," she said, "and I'll lower you to this branch. But hang on to the trunk!"

"Yowl!" the cat struggled, until Ned got a firmer hold on its neck.

"Dratted cat!" came from below. "Oh, children, be careful!"

Ned stepped to her shoulders, and he was heavy. Julie clung to the trunk with an arm and held one of his ankles. Slowly she crouched, until Ned slid off her onto the branch, bumping her head. At that point the cat got away. Puss leaped to the trunk and backed down briskly by herself.

"Oh, bad cat!" The woman smacked her hands, and the cat scatted, tail bushed, to the shed.

"You're sure built right for tree climbing," Ned said gratefully. "Long and skinny."

Julie liked the compliment, except she'd rather he'd said *lean—long and lean.*

First she, then Ned, got themselves down from the tree. On the ground Julie turned to it. "So, ha! tree. We all got away."

"Hmph!" The woman made a sound like a laugh, but said gruffly, "Well—thank you," and looked as though she wanted to smack her hands at the children to scat them, too.

Julie felt suddenly shy with the woman. Yet she'd seemed interested in fairy tales and magic.

"I'm Julie Bennett," she offered, "and this is Ned."

"Ned Pokenberry," he said.

"Really?" Julie turned to him, delighted. "Pokenberry?"

"Yeah. Anybody makes a crack about my name, I give him a poke in the berry!"

Julie laughed.

"Oh." The woman folded the stepladder.

It took Ned's boldness to ask, "What's your name?"

"Fogarty." She dragged the ladder toward the shed, muttering about getting a man to saw off the broken limb.

"Here, Mrs. Fogarty, let me help." Ned picked up one end.

"Miss. Miss Etta Fogarty. Thank you. I can do it. Good-bye."

"Good-bye," Julie said reluctantly. Was there anything magical about the little woman? Probably not.

Just as if she understood what Julie was thinking, Miss Fogarty stopped at the shed door. "Besides fairy tales, do you like ghost stories?"

"I do," Ned said, "and monster stories and—"

"Well"—the woman's face crinkled more with a grin—"the ghost of the girl who used to live next door still climbs in that tree." She popped into the shed, hauling the stepladder after her.

As they went back to the mulberry tree to get their school bags, Ned whispered, "Boy, she's grouchy enough to be a witch! And spooky. Do you suppose she really thinks she's got a ghost for a neighbor?"

Julie was indignant. "She was trying to scare us. So we wouldn't climb this good old tree. That's all the thanks we get!"

That night she asked Dad if he knew anything about Miss Fogarty and her neighbors, but he didn't. He was too new in town. After supper he walked down the street with Julie to see the tree.

"You moved this rock?" He shook his head. "You shouldn't try to heave things like that."

"But it rolled just as easily as if the tree were pulling it! Now it won't move. Try it."

He tugged but could only sway it a few inches between the roots.

"See, it's like magic. It's the magic doorstep to the tree."

"Now, Julie, don't get carried away about magic."

Her father looked up the staircase of branches. "What a tree!" he murmured. Reaching up to the low bough, he swung and chinned himself. But he didn't try to climb the tree, to Julie's relief.

"I had this tree all to myself," she said, "until a boy named Ned started climbing it. He's only a fourth-grader."

Dad smiled at her. "Not eligible to be a friend, hm?"

Julie shrugged. "He'll probably get tired of the tree soon—I hope—and then I won't see much of him."

However, the next day after school she and Ned went back to the tree to prove that they weren't afraid of ghosts. First, though, Ned persuaded Julie to walk up to his house so he could leave his pack and the football he'd taken to school.

"And I ought to check on Silly-Billy."

"What?"

"My twin sisters, Shelley and Bonnie. Bonnie started it, when she couldn't say *Shelley*. Now they're five-year-old punks. Mom had to work this afternoon."

It seemed that his mother cleaned houses for other people in the mornings, after she took the girls to kindergarten; but today she'd gone to an afternoon house. He also had two older half-brothers who would be driving home from high school soon—probably.

Julie wasn't sure she wanted to know that much about Ned Pokenberry and his family. Still, their house interested her. It had old-fashioned big rooms and not a rug or carpet anywhere, so that feet were noisy on the bare floors. But it looked comfortable with the clutter of lots of people living there. A trombone and an electric guitar lay on the tacky vinyl couch in the living room, and the coffee table and floor were littered with magazines, comic books and toys.

It was the first time she had been in someone else's house in Sutterville.

The girls were upstairs playing with an assortment of dolls. Ned looked into their room. "You guys all right?" They nodded and grinned, looking like little female Neds, with their tilted gray-green eyes. "That one's Shelley, and that one is Bonnie." Julie couldn't see an inch of difference in them. "And this is my friend, Julie." Friend, hmph! "I'll be back soon." Ned clattered down the stairs.

Following, Julie said, "Maybe you shouldn't leave them alone, only five years old." She could go to the tree by herself.

"Nah, they'll be all right. When they get tired of

35

dolls, they'll go watch TV. Anyway, here's Hank and Johnny and some guys."

An old clunker of a sedan stopped in front, and four teenagers got out. "Hi, hi, hi you guys, 'bye." They brushed past Ned and Julie into the house.

So they went down the hill to the vacant lot.

"I ought to name this country around the tree," Julie was saying, when she saw something on the mounting rock.

"Cookies!" Ned exclaimed.

On a flatter part of the boulder was a tray of oatmeal cookies covered with plastic wrap. On the ground beside the rock stood a pitcher of lemonade and two paper cups.

"A table spread in the wilderness," Julie murmured, enchanted. In one of her stories a magical table had appeared in the woods, covered with delicious food. She'd always wished it could really happen, and now it had! She pulled the wrap away from the cookies and took one. "Um-yum."

"Wait! Spit it out!" Ned grabbed her hand. "Mom says never take food from strangers. You don't know where this came from. Maybe it's poison."

"It is not poisoned!" A voice came from the other side of the hedge.

"Griselda?" Julie breathed. Of course, who else would— But she was disappointed it wasn't magic, at last.

The little woman hurried around from the alley.

"Here, I'll prove it to you, young smart-alecks! Which one do you want me to eat? Show me, boy."

Now trying not to laugh, Ned pointed out a fat cookie. The woman took it and munched one bite after another.

"There!" She brushed crumbs from her fingers. "I'm not falling over. Satisfied? Just thought you nuisances would be hungry after school."

"Oh, Miss Fogarty, thank you!" Julie said. "It was like magic to see the food here, out of nowhere." She poured some lemonade into a cup.

"Takes more than a fairy wand to make oatmeal cookies," the woman gruffed. "But I pay my debts. Don't expect this again."

"Well, thanks for today, anyway," Ned said cheerily, eating. "How's your cat?"

"Fine. Watch out for the ghost." Miss Fogarty trotted toward the alley, turning to say, "Leave the pitcher and the tray on my front porch, girl."

"What's her name, the ghost?" Julie called after her.

"Gracie. Gracie Wolcott." The woman disappeared along the alley.

"Good grief! A ghost that even has a last name." Julie put two cookies in her shirt pocket and swung up into the tree. "I'm first in my tower room. You can pilot your boat later."

"Okay." Ned helped himself to lemonade and another cookie.

Julie wanted to be alone to think about all this. In the top of the tree she ate a cookie, spicy and still warm. It would have tasted even better if Miss Etta Fogarty could have been more friendly about her gift. What a prickly old woman! I'm never going to get like that, Julie thought. Looking down into the garden, she saw nothing of the woman or her cat. The pear tree branch still dangled, broken.

Julie finished the second cookie. Too bad it wasn't magic. She wondered what a real magic cookie would taste like. Relaxed against a branch in the tower, she noticed a few leaves were getting dry and rattly, no longer glossy green. And a flick of redness showed on a treetop near a church steeple. True, it was the last week in September. In another month she could be climbing among beautiful autumn leaves. Would there be reds and yellows in the mulberry tree? She hoped the leaves wouldn't just turn brown and fall off.

Would she be rid of Ned by then? Did she want to be? And was there really a ghost? She ought to come here on Halloween night and watch. I will, she decided. Would she be afraid to watch alone?

"My turn." Ned came climbing up the tree, managing to clatter.

"Now don't break a branch on this one!" Julie cautioned him. She moved down to let him up into his pilot house and leaned against the trunk. "Hear that clack-clack? I wonder what that factory makes."

"I know. Are you ready? They make curry combs, hog rings and turkey bits!" He grinned, nodding.

"Wha-at? What *are* those things?"

"Well, there's farm country around town," Ned explained. "The curry combs are to curry horses, brush them. The hog rings they put in hogs' noses to keep them from rooting up vegetables. And the turkey bits they put in the turkeys' mouths, when they're going to ride them in races."

"When they *ride* the turkeys? Come on!" She saw Ned's grin. For some reason Julie loved to be teased, when it wasn't mean teasing. She laughed. "You nut! What do they really—"

"Hey, you kids, get outta that tree!"

The shout came from a heavy teenaged boy walking across the street from the factory. Julie and Ned silently blended against the trunk. The kid came into the vacant lot and walked toward the tree, shading his eyes against the sun.

"Get down from there, before you fall down!" he yelled.

"We're all right," Julie tried.

But Ned demanded, "Is this your tree?"

"Naw, it's nobody's tree—anybody's tree. So I got a right to tell you to get out of it." He stood planted, hands thrust into black jacket pockets. "So come on down. I'm waiting."

Julie exclaimed, "If it's anybody's tree, then we've got a right to stay here! Go away!" That was the way Mom would speak up bravely. Sometimes she could do it, too.

"All right, but I'm gonna report you!" He turned toward the parking area.

"Report us to who?" Ned muttered and yelled, "To who?"

Unexpectedly, Julie laughed. "You sound like an owl in a tree, *to-who, to-whooo*."

So they called that at the bully, *To-who, to-whooo!* But he got on a motorcycle, started it and drowned them out. He sat there gunning the engine for a long time, making so much noise they couldn't hear the *clack* of the factory. Then he *vroom*ed away.

Julie started to climb down. "I hope he doesn't report us."

"I bet he doesn't. Just being a pest."

She wasn't so sure. As she gathered up Miss Fogarty's things, Julie felt niggles of worry. Here she'd thought she had found a wild private place and her own best climbing tree. They were about as private as a playground at recess.

.

4

"I'm not ready for a stepmother!"

"Oh, nonsense, Julie! I hardly know her. There's not much conversation when you're jogging."

That morning Dad had brought a young woman in for breakfast. Her name was Joella; she lived in the apartment house at the other end of the block; and it seemed she'd been jogging the same route with Dad for several weeks. It was the first Julie had known of the person. Julie could see that even though she wore baggy sweatpants, Joella was a scrawny thing with hair all scraped back from her face.

Betsy Bennett had been a big beautiful woman, and so was Frannie. One time Dad had said he felt like a skinny mutt chasing after two tricolor collies. Well, now he was running with another mutt!

When Joella said bagels and cream cheese were a good idea for breakfast, Julie only nodded. When Dad said Joella was a dental assistant, Julie grimaced. Probably all the woman did was clean teeth. When Joella said she had to go get ready for work, Julie took the plates to the sink.

"I was sorry to see you act so rude to her," Dad said.

That's when Julie challenged him about a stepmother, and it went on, while they washed dishes, until Julie accused him, "You could have told me about her. You kept her a secret until now on purpose!"

Dad threw the dishcloth in the water so hard it splashed. "I can't talk to you if you're going to be unreasonable." He clammed up, the way he used to with Mom.

Julie walked to the school bus with a nervous stomach. She'd almost never quarreled with Dad. How could he act like that toward her? What would happen to her, if Dad got married again?

The day, having started badly, of course continued that way. At the bus stop Ned said, "I can't go to the tree with you this afternoon, because I have to go to Scouts." He was wearing a Cub Scout shirt.

Not even bothering to whisper, Sandy said to two

other girls, "Julie Bennett has a cute little boyfriend in uniform," and the three snickered.

"Stick it in your ear," Ned told Sandy.

She obeyed by sticking both thumbs in her ears, waggling her fingers and putting out her tongue at him.

The bus had come. Starting up the steps, Ned called back, "Keep it up. Makes you look like a horse's tail." He shoved down the aisle to sit with a boy.

During art class one of Sandy's buddies, Becca, was next to Julie while they were getting supplies. Becca was a cheerful person. She asked, "What tree was that kid talking about?"

Even though the girl acted friendly, Julie was cautious. "Just a tree."

"But—" Becca looked puzzled. "Why do you go to a tree?"

"Well." Julie shrugged. "It's a good climbing tree."

She watched Becca for the giggles, but the girl said, "Oh. I used to climb trees." Her voice was thoughtful, not a put-down.

Julie almost asked if Becca still liked to climb trees, but she didn't. The tree ought to be a secret. What if Becca told Sandy, and they teased her?

They didn't, because they went to an after-school club instead of coming on the bus. And with Ned at Scouts, at least she'd have the tree all to herself. She could roam the tree wherever she wanted, without Ned crashing around.

First she rocked herself on the front porch bough, and then she tried climbing with her eyes shut. Her hands and feet did reach to the right places, pretty much, until she got to the living room, but after that, she'd forgotten the steps to the top. Eyes open, she looked out over the rooftops outlined in squares by the green treetops.

She wondered which streets Dad and Joella jogged. Their faces had been happy when they came in, breathless and laughing. Then she'd acted sour as a grapefruit. Thinking about them, she still felt sour.

Julie climbed down a little way to a place where the trunk divided. There was a set of branches, like a side attic, that she hadn't explored yet. Edging along a limb, she sat as far out as she dared. Dad *would* care, if she fell out of the tree. . . . No! She wouldn't think about him.

It couldn't be true, could it, that the ghost of a girl still climbed the tree? Sometimes when she'd thought she heard Squirrel rustling around, could it have been the ghost? Gracie Wolcott. It made it more real that the ghost had a full name. Cinderella didn't have a last name. In fairy tales a lot of the girls didn't even have first names. Julie ran a finger along the sawtooth edge of a leaf, as she wondered what Gracie Wolcott had looked like.

Something flapped above and settled on a top branch, making it dip. Did ghosts flap? Oh, horrors, in thinking about Gracie had she summoned the ghost?

Carefully, heart pounding, Julie moved to see past leaves to the thing above her. It was black, not ghostly white. It was a crow.

"Caw, caw!" the crow croaked at her movement. It lifted its wings for a moment, then flew away.

Julie let out her breath. Only a bird. Yet the black figure of the crow had been eerie, too. The way it hooded up its wings . . . maybe Gracie could turn into a crow— Ah, come on, quit scaring yourself, she scolded. Quit thinking about ghosts. It was Griselda's fault, Miss Fogarty's fault, for telling her.

Looking toward the house, Julie saw a face at an upper window. The woman was watching her. After everything else! Julie made an angry pushing motion toward her. She didn't *want* to be watched. At once the face disappeared.

Julie stepped down to the friendlier crotch of branches where Squirrel's hollow was. She breathed in huffs. Bad. Everything was bad. If that woman came out in the yard, she'd just tell her!

Soon the screen door flapped, and Miss Fogarty came out wearing garden gloves and carrying a trowel. Julie hurried down from the tree and ran around through the alley.

45

Over the back gate she called, "Why were you watching me?"

The little woman knelt at some bare earth and was digging bulbs out of it. "Mff." She hunched around to see Julie. "I need to watch, in case one of you children falls out of the tree."

"I'm not going to fall!" Julie snapped. "I never have."

But some of the steam had gone out of her. Maybe the woman really did worry. Julie backed down from demanding, *Quit watching me!* Instead, she changed the subject. "Is that tree really a mulberry tree? I mean, I didn't know they got so big."

"Of course it's a mulberry tree. I don't know how it managed to grow so tall. Some do. Good soil, maybe." Miss Fogarty moved on her knees to trowel up more earth and bulbs. "It was a good-sized tree when I was a girl."

"You've lived next door to this tree all your life?" Julie didn't think she liked that. It made the tree almost more the woman's than hers.

"Most of my life," the woman was muttering. "I used to climb in that tree with Gracie."

So Gracie was real, someone this woman had known. Julie pictured two girls in long skirts and white pinafores. "In long dresses? How could—"

"How old do you think I am?" Miss Fogarty wheeled around crossly. "We wore pants, same as you, when we did things like that. Even fifty, no, sixty years ago." Her voice trailed off, as she turned back to the earth.

Julie stood there trying to realize it: the tree had been good sized that long ago, plenty big enough for climbing. What on earth was the tree's age?

"There isn't really a ghost, is there?" she asked.

The woman looked over her shoulder. "Haven't you left yet? Ghost?" She shrugged. "If you don't want me watching you, stop watching me. Run along."

Dismissed like a little child, Julie drag-footed back to the vacant lot. Why did that wonderful tree have to be planted next door to a witch!

Anyway, it was too late in the day for any more climbing. She followed the path, eyeing the foundation remains of the house where Gracie Wolcott had lived. At the back there must have been a garden, for white daisies scattered wild in the grass. As she crossed the street toward the factory, the teenaged boy came out, pulling on his black jacket.

"Hey!" He recognized her. "You want to know who I reported you to, smarty? I mentioned you kids to the foreman. And you know what he said?"

Julie couldn't move, couldn't look away from his heavy face. There were three angry red swellings on his skin and two scarred pits.

"He said that property over there belongs to the

city. And they wouldn't want you messing around in that tree, in case you fell out and sued the city. So—"

He went on, but she put her hands over her ears. She wouldn't hear what he was saying. She wouldn't let the words go from her ears to her mind.

Julie hurried to get to her house before it happened. She fumbled the key in the lock and opened the door at last. As she climbed the stairs to her room, the sobs broke out. They were painful, tearing at her throat, after holding in so long.

"Ohhhh," she let out a long wail and fell on her bed. Tears wet her face. "Oh, oh, oh!" she cried against the pillow. The more she cried, the more she had to.

The back door opened, closed . . . footsteps on the stairs. Julie gulped, but the next sob erupted. "Oh!"

Dad came into her room. "What are you crying about?"

She hid her face from him. "Everything!" she wailed.

"Ah, Julie, it's not so bad." He sat beside her and rubbed her back. "Is it about Joella?"

"That, too." Another sob shook her.

"It was only a spur-of-the-moment idea, but you were right. I shouldn't have sprung her on you without notice." His voice pleaded, "Julie, look at me."

He tried to turn her over, but she resisted. He kept on massaging her shoulders to ease them.

He does care, Julie thought. Usually he didn't try to straighten out quarrels.

"Are you going to marry her?" she asked, voice muffled.

"Don't know her well enough. But look, Julie, not all stepmothers are wicked, any more than all godmothers are fairies."

Julie rolled over and saw his kind face. "Who's my godmother? Have I got a godmother?"

"Yes, my sister Margo. But that's not the point. The thing is, not only do you need to make new friends here, but so do I. You don't want to stop me from having friends, do you?"

"Well, I haven't made any friends," Julie burst out on a sob. "My only friend is a tree. And they're trying to take that away from me!"

"Who's *they*?"

She sat up and told about the teenaged bully and what he had said. "They're going to make me stop climbing the tree. I just know it!"

To her dismay Dad said, "That could happen. The city government wouldn't want to be responsible for medical bills, if someone got hurt."

Julie had forgotten that Dad always took things seriously. If it had been Mom, she would have comforted, "Never happen, honey." She would have just told that kid to buzz off. Which he had, on his motorcycle. Julie almost smiled, sniffing.

But there she went again, not facing the problem. She didn't know whether the factory foreman had told the city people, because she had quit listening to the teenager. She kept backing off from problems, the same way Dad did.

"What are we going to do?" she insisted. Her eyes stung from crying, and more tears washed them.

"I don't know." Dad picked up one of her hands, murmuring, "So scuffed up." He turned it over to see the palm. "Anyone would know you've been climbing a tree—or hauling ropes."

Was he trying to slide away from this, too? "Maybe if I went to the city people and asked permission?"

"No. Let me think about it." He got up and looked out the gable window, then turned back. "We both recognize that boy was bent on tormenting you. But unless somebody official tells you not to climb the tree, I guess you can do it. If an official speaks up, we'll face that then."

There. He hadn't said useless things like *I'll beat up that bully.* Or *Forget the tree and make real friends.* He'd spelled out the situation clearly and honestly.

Julie gave a sigh that relaxed her. It was a relief, anyway, to see how things stood.

5

In the night the sky flashed and crashed and sent down rain. The rain continued, and for two days the tree was left to itself. Julie didn't follow the path, for the high wet grass along it would have drenched her.

At school she volunteered to help make posters for the hallways; she talked to kids and played Ping-Pong one noon hour with a girl named Carrie; she was doing her best to fit in, she told herself. But there was no progress in making any special friends. Carrie lived too far out in the country on a farm for Julie to see anything of her outside of school.

Once, as Ned came racing through the halls, she tried to tell him what the teenager had said about the tree and the city officials. However, he was busy punching with another boy.

Then, in the following days, it seemed everyone wanted to visit the mulberry tree!

Saturday morning the sky was clear. A light wind blew cool. First Julie went to the library—it had old-fashioned fairy tale books the school library didn't have—and then she went to the tree. She found people there. A multitude around the boulder!

No, as she got closer, she saw most of them were dolls and toy animals. The two live ones were Silly-Billy. Ned was stretched out on his stomach on the long bough above them.

"Hey!" he called gladly, sitting up.

"What?" Julie gestured at the girls and the twin doll strollers that had carried the crowd.

"I had to bring them. Mom's working, and the guys are gone. Come on up."

Julie saw leaves had blown off the tree, and the girls had placed them as green plates in front of each doll and animal. The scene was so pleasant that Julie was ashamed of the whiff of resentment she'd felt about the girls.

She asked one of them, "Are you Shelley?"

The twin glanced sideways from her tilted eyes. "She's Shelley. I'm Bonnie."

Studying the girls, Julie decided Shelley's cheeks were a shade thinner, and her eyes were more flecked with gray, while Bonnie's eyes were a clearer green.

"Okay, let me test," Julie said. "You two run around the tree, while I close my eyes, and then let me see if I can tell you apart."

The girls shrieked into the game, chasing around the tree, until Julie called, "Stop." They fell in a heap, laughing, but she sorted out one girl.

"You're Bonnie."

The twin giggled and shook her head. "I'm Shelley."

"We're Silly-Billy," the other one said.

"Hey, you guys, cut it out," Ned ordered from the limb above. "Julie, you were right. They do that, try to keep people mixed up."

Julie stared at the twin imps. "Don't each of you want to be your own self?"

Shelley hesitated, but Bonnie—if she had them right—said firmly, "No, we're Silly-Billy." They went back to their dolls.

Julie tried once more. "What are your dolls' names?"

They both said, "Charlene," so she gave it up.

She climbed up and sat on the bough beside Ned. "There's trouble," she said. "That kid from the factory did report us." She repeated what he'd said about the city officials.

"Aw, they wouldn't tell us not to climb here,

53

would they?" Ned bounced the bough, making drops of water spatter down on his sisters. They squeaked protest, so he bounced again. "If they did, what could we do?"

"I don't know."

Ned looked up through the branches. "Well, if they do, I'll miss this tree."

Julie realized she would miss Ned, too. At school they went their own ways; the only thing they had in common was the tree.

"I'm not giving up so easily!" she exclaimed. "You be thinking, too, what we could do."

"Okay. Can you do this?" Hooking his knees tight to the bough, Ned dropped back and hung by his knees.

"Sure." Julie wondered if she would fall *plock* on her head, but she anchored her knees and let go with her hands when she was almost hanging down. They must look like monkeys, hanging side by side from the branch.

"Neat, huh? How high up in the tree would you hang by your knees?" Ned dared her.

"Not one branch higher!" She refused the dare.

Looking up through the branches, she thought how strange and new the tree was, seen from upside down. She felt a tug on her longish hair hanging down and saw one of the girls—Shelley?—standing up to look into her face. Shelley's eyes looked out from above her hair, and her mouth seemed to be at the top of her head.

"You look funny!" they said together.

"Your face is red," Shelley added.

Laughing, Julie managed to pull herself back up on the bough. "Come on," she said to Ned. "You're turning purple. You want to pilot the River Queen today?"

Of course he did. He scrambled above her to the top branches, and Julie began pretending the riverboat was carrying a load of toys down on the cargo deck.

"And we're bringing her clear up from New Orleans," Ned joined in, "except we're attacked by river pirates!"

"And we shoot our cannon!" Julie flopped a limber limb, volleying leaves. "Pow! Pow!"

But the pirates swarmed aboard, and Julie had to do some tricky steering of the boat, while Ned fought off the pirates in hand-to-hand combat. At last they sank the pirates' boat with accurate shots of the cannon.

Then Ned cried, "Oh, no! A river witch is sailing up on our right! Starboard, I mean."

Julie saw Miss Fogarty coming along the sidewalk with a large grocery sack. She walked slowly, as if she were tired.

"I'll take care of the witch Griselda," Julie announced.

She climbed down and ran around to Miss Fogarty's front walk. "Can I help?" She held the grocery sack, while Miss Fogarty dug her door key out of her purse.

"What are all those children doing over there?" she asked crossly. "Do you have to keep bringing more?" She took the sack.

"They're Ned's sisters," Julie began, but Griselda went inside and shut the door. No thanks from the river witch!

Ned had climbed down, too. "Let's go, girls. I'm hungry for lunch."

"Okay." They began stacking dolls and animals in the strollers. " 'Bye, tree. We'll be back."

"Oh, yeah?" Julie said.

Ned grinned at her, looking just as impish as the twins.

She didn't know if they came back Sunday, because that day she went with her father to a fish fry at the boat club down on the river. There were people Dad worked with but no children her age, only a baby in a stroller and two teenaged boys. Julie sat on the riverbank and watched a towboat sweep down the Mississippi pushing covered barges, and she dipped her feet in the chilly river. It was the first day of October.

She wondered if she'd swim in the river next summer. Splashing and racing with kids—but who? In late winter, swim classes started at the indoor pool

at the Y. Surely, by next summer she'd be swimming with somebody.

On Monday Julie took Becca to the tree. It was Becca who brought up the idea, while they worked on the hall posters.

"You still climbing some tree?" she asked. "I wish I could try climbing it. I haven't been up in a tree for a long time."

"Well—um—sure," Julie said, making time, while she thought fast. Did she want yet another person in her tree? What would Ned think? But she had the impulse to feel closer to this friendly girl. Becca reminded her a little of Amy.

"Okay, after school I'll show you. Would Sandy want to come?" Oh, too many people!

But no, Sandy was going to the dentist after school, Becca said.

So the two girls got off the school bus together and started down Fourth Street. Ned jogged after them.

"What are you doing?"

"Uh—Becca wants to see the tree." Julie nodded toward Ned. "Becca, you know Ned Pokenberry?"

"Well—gee!" He stuck his hands in his back jeans pockets. "That's our tree."

"So? I'm not going to eat it," Becca said, smiling.

"You brought Silly-Billy," Julie pointed out.

"That's different."

But instead of turning away, Ned came grumbling along, and Julie grinned. Now he knew how she'd felt!

Under the tree Becca exclaimed, "Oh, what a wonderful old tree! You can't tell from the street. No wonder you like it."

Julie beamed at the appreciation for "her" tree, but Ned sat on the ground glumly plucking at grass.

"Okay, go on," he said. "Let's see how good you can climb."

"All right, but Julie, you go first. Don't look up," Becca told Ned, giggling. She was wearing a denim skirt.

"Aw, who'd want to!" He looked away in disgust.

Julie climbed as far as the elbow branch in back. "See, the limbs are like stair steps to follow," she began, feeling as though she was leading a tour.

Becca pulled herself up to the crotch a bit awkwardly and stepped on her skirt. Julie caught her breath, as Becca teetered and recovered. Julie always wore jeans and hadn't thought about the skirt being a problem. This girl better not ruin everything by falling out of the tree! However, Becca climbed sturdily enough after Julie and managed to get herself clear to the top in the tower room.

Looking out, she cried, "Oh, look at all this! I love it!"

In that moment Julie thought, Yes! Maybe this girl could be a friend.

Coming down was harder for Becca. She kept stepping on the skirt and laughing at herself. Then the skirt snagged on a branch. Becca couldn't twist around far enough to reach it, and Julie had to climb up and unhook it.

From below, Ned called, "Fall here!" He'd gathered a big clump of grass. "No, here," he shifted the pillow of grass, as Becca backed around the trunk. She slipped and caught herself. "Oh, I see you want to fall there. Okay, booby, I'll catch you." He whopped the grass around.

"Silly!"

"Nut!"

The girls laughed at his foolishness and stopped to rest in the living-room branches.

Becca whispered, "He's jealous of me being here. Is he really your boyfriend?"

Julie laughed. "Him? Good grief!"

Ned looked up at them suspiciously. "Now what are you stupids giggling about?"

"You!"

"Aw, giggling girls are like chattering squirrels!"

That made them giggle more. Ordinarily Julie wasn't a giggling person, so it felt extra good to be laughing with a girl again.

When Ned came swarming up the tree, she pretended to shiver and cried, "Oo, he's going to attack," and the girls laughed.

Instead, he stepped on past them and climbed to

the top branches, where he perched and chanted, "Giggling girls are chattering squirrels! Giggling—" He stopped. "Hey, she's watching."

Julie looked next door. Nobody in the back yard. Then she saw Miss Fogarty's face at the upper window. Still in the happy mood, Julie waved. The face didn't move.

"Wave!" she called to Ned, and he did.

"Who? What?" Becca was asking.

There was the flicker of a hand at the window. It made Julie feel good. It was okay to be watched by a friendly Miss Fogarty. Julie waved again. For some reason, though, she didn't explain to Becca.

The next day Becca called, " 'Bye, see you," to Julie, when they got off the school bus, and she walked away with Sandy.

Julie turned to Ned, "You going to the tree?"

"No." He started to walk away, too.

"Hey, are you mad?"

"No." Then he stopped and smiled. "Maybe a little. You acted so silly with that girl. But really, I've got to catch up on some homework."

Walking down the hill, Julie decided maybe she'd better spend some time on homework, too. If she climbed the tree every day, it wouldn't be special anymore. As Frannie said about things getting old, it would start to taste like paint. However, she wished she could talk to Miss Fogarty for a minute.

Julie walked along the alley and looked through the wire fence. Nobody in the back yard except the cat, rustling some fallen pear leaves. She was about to go on, when the little woman came out of the shed carrying a red clay pot.

"Hello," Julie said.

Miss Fogarty nearly dropped the pot. "Oh, merciful heavens, you startled me! Why are you sneaking around?"

"I'm not!" Julie flared. "Any more than you were spying yesterday." Goodness, she didn't know she was going to sound so smarty.

But a smile creased the tough old face. "Maybe I was." Then she said severely, "Bringing one child after another to that tree—what next, a bus tour?"

Not seeming to expect an answer, she began to dig a tomato plant out of the ground by the fence.

After a moment Julie said, "I wanted to tell you something. Today at school I read about mulberry trees, and it said sometimes the root system gets as big as the treetop!"

They both looked at the mulberry branches, picturing that many roots spreading underground.

"Amazing!" Miss Fogarty whispered.

Julie said, "Maybe some roots even reach under your yard."

The woman looked at the earth under her trowel. "Maybe. Never dug down to any." She lifted the tomato plant into the large pot.

More shyly Julie asked, "Um—I was wondering, did you and Gracie ever name that tree?"

Miss Fogarty grinned at the dirt she was sifting around the tomato plant roots. "Yes. Mabel."

"Mabel!" Julie laughed. She had expected something poetic, like *Lofty*.

The lady husked her dry laugh, too. "Mabel Mulberry. We thought it was funny, Gracie and I."

Imagining two girls laughing in the tree, Julie felt safe to tell her, "I call it the Armstrong Apartments." She explained about the rooms of the tree and the squirrels and birds living in it, but not the part about the strong arms.

Miss Fogarty nodded. "Yes, it could be."

"I was wondering, too," Julie went on, "what did she look like? Gracie."

"Hm." Miss Fogarty troweled loose dirt in the hole, then glanced at Julie. "Hm! Something like you. Lanky, same kind of long face, same brown hair, except hers was bobbed short."

Julie was disappointed. She'd been picturing Gracie with a pretty face and long wavy yellow hair pulled back by a ribbon. She tried to imagine how Etta Fogarty had looked, but all she could see was a tough little face with a pert nose.

There was something else she wanted to know about Gracie, but today was going so well with the old lady that she decided not to chance spoiling it.

"Well, I have to go now. Unless you need help carrying the pot."

"No." The small woman picked it up, as if she. were strong as a troll.

Julie went on through the alley. She wondered if Dad and Joella ever jogged there. Saturday night they all were going to a movie. Dad had said an old Charlie Chaplin film was showing downtown, and Joella wanted to see it, too. He'd asked Julie to come. And she'd said *yes*, because she certainly wasn't going to let them go alone!

The next afternoon Becca and Sandy went to their after-school club, and Ned was off to Cub Scouts. As Julie started along the path, she tried to think of the right name for this place of yellowing grass and secret hollows. A wilderness. Wilder-land? Maybe. Then she saw there was somebody at the tree. Not a child, a taller person. Black jacket . . . it was the boy from the factory.

Julie stopped and almost went back. Then she went on. She had a right here. If he told her something awful—she might as well know it.

However, as she got closer, the boy reached up to the long bough and laboriously pulled himself up, trying to chin himself. Heavy though he was, he made it and dropped down again as Julie came by, not leaving the path.

"Bet you can't do that!" he challenged her.

Of course she couldn't. Even though she was tall for her age, she could barely brush the bough with her fingertips, when she'd jumped up once.

"No." Was he going to tell some bad news?

Instead he pulled himself up again, showing off.

"How come you're not in school?" she asked.

"Work release. I get to the factory"—he sucked breath—"at two thirty."

"What's your name?"

"Chester!" he puffed, coming down.

Chester. Not a popular name. Suddenly she wondered if any of the kids his age liked him. . . . Don't go feeling sorry for him!

" 'Bye," she said, walking on. She hunched her shoulders, in case he called something mean at her back, but he didn't. As she walked on up Jefferson Street, she heard his motorcycle revving.

The next day one more person came to the tree. Julie and Ned were starting down the hill, when Becca called behind them, "Wait up. Sandy wants to see the tree."

Julie's heart gave a big thump. She saw both girls were wearing jeans, which hadn't really registered before. Why couldn't they have given her warning at school?

"Yeah, I'm an old tree-climber from way back," Sandy said, grinning.

64

"Well—" Julie said, as the girls caught up.

"Aw, no!" Ned exclaimed. "Not a *bunch* of girls!"

Becca giggled and Sandy gave her *e-yuck* laugh. She said to Julie, "You show me your tree, and I might show you mine. There's a good maple in our back yard."

"Okay!" Julie led the way to the path.

Ned hesitated behind them, saying, "Yeah, but—" and Julie thought maybe he'd go home. Then she was ashamed of herself.

"Does he have to tag along?" Sandy muttered loud enough for him to hear.

That decided Ned. "No! Because I'm ahead of you!" He raced down the path and leaped up into the tree, scattering twigs in his hurry to get to the top.

"He's weird," Sandy said. "I've seen Ned Pokenberry for years, and you don't want to hang around with that kid," she told Julie. "However," she looked up the tree, "yeah, this is a terrific tree. Handy that rock's there, too."

She climbed up without being invited.

"If you swing around—" Julie began, but Sandy was already shinnying up the trunk a different way. "You go on," Julie said politely to Becca. With Sandy here she didn't feel the same giggly friendliness they'd shared the other day.

She'd wanted to be friends with Sandy first, be-cause Sandy was funny and lively. Now it was as

65

if Becca came between them. And Ned was yelling, "Caw! Caw!" from the treetop for some crazy reason.

Too many people! She didn't know how to be friends with more than one person at a time.

Julie climbed the staircase of branches, but Becca, trying to follow Sandy's different route, was in trouble.

"Ow!" she cried, as bark scraped her hands, when she slipped down the trunk she was gripping.

Julie gave her a boost from below. "Step around here," she advised.

She could see Sandy climbed expertly enough, even if she didn't have any feeling for the pattern of the tree. Sandy did follow the natural inclination, though, to rest in the branches at the stair landing.

"Hey, you know what?" she called. "There's a squirrel in this hole!"

She reached in and pulled him out, but Squirrel flipped out of her hand and rippled out on a branch. There he set up a fearful screeching.

Becca gasped, "Did he bite you?" and Sandy snorted, "No."

Julie didn't know what to think. Sandy certainly was brave to grab a squirrel like that. Yet—to grab Squirrel—it didn't seem right.

Becca reached the landing, as Sandy started moving up. Julie followed, wondering when they were going to have a traffic jam.

"Hey, funny man at the top!" Sandy called. "Come down out of the way, so I can see what it's like up there."

"No. I got here first." Ned swayed the top branches in defiance.

"Julie," Sandy demanded, "make him come down."

"Caw! Caw!" Ned croaked.

"Well—well," Julie stuttered, "I can't make him."

"Sure you can. He's just a little kid. Tell him."

Julie tried to slide away from it. "See that branch you're on, Sandy? If you go out on it, you're like in a side attic."

Sandy shifted her feet on the limb. "No, I want to go up there. Look," she challenged, "who do you want to be friends with, that weirdo or me?"

All the noise in the tree—Ned crowing, Squirrel chattering, Becca giggling nervously and Sandy yelling at her—Julie couldn't stand it.

"He's not a weirdo!" she cried. "And he's not just a little kid, either. If you asked him nice, maybe he'd—"

"Forget it! I'm coming down!" Sandy plunged off the branch, grabbing the trunk.

At the same time Becca said, "There's a woman watching us."

Julie saw Miss Fogarty in the back yard below, and her face wore a definite scowl.

Then Sandy fell.

6

As Sandy pushed past Becca, her foot missed the next branch, and she came scraping down the trunk, gasping, "Ow! Oh!"

Julie snatched at her body and broke her fall but couldn't hold her. Sliding down, Sandy grabbed the limb Julie was on, and nearly knocked her off it. Sandy careened on down the tree, helter-skelter, slipping and catching herself. At last near the bottom crotch she fell *whop* on the ground.

In an instant of silence Julie heard Potter's factory beating *clack-clack-ti-clack-clack*. Then Sandy got her breath and let out a loud *wahh* of crying.

The others hurried down the tree, Becca exclaiming, "Oh, Sandy! Oh, poor Sandy!" Ned called,

"I'm sorry! I didn't make her do it. Did I?" Julie didn't say anything until she got down to Sandy and heard herself asking the usual idiotic "Are you all right?"

Of course Sandy wasn't. Her arms were skinned up, and blood showed through her torn jeans at one knee. She stayed crumpled on the ground and sobbed heartily.

Miss Fogarty came running from the alley, crying, "I knew it! Oh dear!"

Once Julie had read of a witch ill-wishing someone by giving that person the evil eye.

But Julie couldn't think of Miss Fogarty as a witch when the woman knelt by Sandy, saying, "Now, now, of course it hurts. See if you can move your arms, your legs."

Sandy uncrumpled herself. "Everybody leave me alone! I'm all right!"

"Can you walk to my house?" Miss Fogarty asked. "I'll take care of your scrapes." She tried to lift Sandy.

"No!" Sandy got up. "Oh, my hip! My shoulder!" She rubbed the sore places. "No! I'm going home! Come on, Becca."

"How far—" Julie began.

But Sandy insisted on hobbling up the path, leaning on Becca, who looked back once, sighing and shaking her head.

"I knew somebody was going to fall out of that tree!" Miss Fogarty exclaimed. "When I heard all that hollering." She looked at Julie and Ned. "Are you two all right?"

"Yes," they agreed.

"Then it's time everybody went home."

So they did.

The next day Sandy said nothing at all to Julie on the bus or at school. When Julie tried to ask how she was, Sandy only looked the other way.

In the girls' restroom Becca whispered to Julie, "She'll be okay. I think she's embarrassed because she fell. And because we all saw her crying."

"Good grief! Anybody would!"

After school Julie and Ned drifted down to the tree, very subdued. They climbed to the first bough and sat there, side by side.

"I don't feel like going up," Julie said.

"Me neither." Ned was too glum even to bounce the bough. He said, "Thanks for—you know—yesterday. What you said to her about me."

"Sure. Only fair."

"I guess maybe I should have let her—"

"Well—" Looking up, Julie saw a small limb hanging broken, but she didn't feel like doing anything about it.

A voice spoke from beyond the hedge. "I'm not spreading any more tables in the wilderness, but if you want cookies, come over."

Julie and Ned brightened, looking at each other. "Come in the front door," Miss Fogarty's voice added. "I'm scrubbing the floor at the back entry."

The blue-eyed cat met them on the porch and smoothed against their legs, while Julie knocked on the screen door. The wooden door beyond stood open, showing a dark hallway.

"Come in," Miss Fogarty called from the back of the house. "I said, come in!"

Julie hesitated. "Should we? She's coaxing us in with cookies," she murmured. "Remember the witch and the goodies in 'Hansel and Gretel'?"

"What's that?" Ned peered nervously at the shadowed interior.

"You know, the gingerbread house? The witch put Hansel in a cage and fed him to fatten him up. Remember, to cook him in her oven."

"Ah, you know too much." As Julie stepped over the doorsill, Ned stuck out his foot and tripped her, grabbing her elbow to steady her, all the time grinning.

In a front room off the hall Julie saw a three-cornered glass-sided cabinet filled with painted china and shimmering silver. Something touched her leg, and Julie started, but it was only the softness of the cat, which had slid through the doorway with them. There was a sharp spicy smell pricking the air. And lemon.

When she and Ned followed the hallway back, Julie saw why. On the kitchen table were pans of warm lemon cookies and molasses cookies.

"Two kinds!" Ned whispered.

Miss Fogarty came in from the back entry. She sat them down at the table and put cookies on napkins in front of them.

Julie said, "I saw some beautiful china in your cabinet. Do you ever use it? Oh, um!" She had taken a bite of molasses cookie, and now there were pinpricks of spiciness in her mouth.

"Only when it's my turn to have the Altar Guild here," Miss Fogarty said, taking another pan out of the oven. "Which is tomorrow noon. That's why I made cookies."

Not for her and Ned, then. Hearing about Altar Guild made it awfully hard to think of the small woman as either a witch or an elf lady.

"Which church do you go to?" Julie asked.

"St. Mark's." She hitched a shoulder in the direction of one of the church spires.

Was there no mystery about this woman, after all? Julie said, "I don't understand something. How can you see us through the hedge, when we can't see you?"

The woman glanced out a window toward the hedge, which showed just as thick on this side. "I wove a spell on it. That's my magic hedge to protect me."

Julie and Ned looked at each other.

Miss Fogarty sat down at the table with them. "It's like the roadhouses in the old days that had one-way windows," she said. "The owner of the cafe could look out the window to see who was there, but all the person outside saw was a mirror in the door. Same with my hedge." Wrinkles tucked in around the corners of her mouth, that sly smile.

"You're kidding!" Ned decided.

"Who knows?" The woman shrugged. "It protects me."

Ned helped himself to another molasses cookie. "One time there was a storyteller at the library like you," he said. "Did you use to be a librarian?"

"Far from it! I worked in the County Assessor's office, and then I was City Clerk for years."

It sounded like an important job, but it was more everydayness that couldn't have to do with magic. Still, there was the ghost.

"How did Gracie Wolcott die? Did she fall out of the tree?"

Julie didn't mean to blurt it out like that, and she knew she shouldn't have. She'd shocked the woman. The face went old and cold.

"Please. I'm sorry. But I worry—"

"Oh, child." Miss Fogarty wiped her hand over her face, pulling back the toughness. "No, she didn't fall out of the tree. Not her!"

Julie waited. Ned kicked her foot under the table, shaking his head.

But the woman did answer her. "She died of pneumonia, when she was thirteen. We were skating on a pond, and she went through the ice. Too cold. Too young."

In the silence Ned crunched on a thin lemon cookie and quickly put it down. Julie couldn't finish the one in her hand.

"I'm sorry I—" she whispered.

"So there isn't any ghost?" Ned asked.

"I didn't say that. When she was in bed shaking with the fever," the woman's voice mused, as if to herself, "she looked toward her window and said, *Tree, I'll climb you again.*"

In the next silence the cat's purr throbbed somewhere near. Julie had looked away from Miss Fogarty's face, because it was too private to watch. Did the woman really think—

"Now this is what," Miss Fogarty said, suddenly brisk. "My hedge may shelter me a bit, but not from swarms of people. Every day for the past week there's been somebody new on the other side. I want to ask you two to stop bringing children to that tree."

Julie felt shaken, then a hot dart of anger. These switches were too much for her, the way the woman kept switching from niceness to meanness. There she'd been feeling close and sympathetic to the old lady—and now here was the real reason she'd invited them in for cookies. She wasn't being friendly, after all. Don't bring Becca. Or Sandy. Don't come.

"I guess you wish Ned and I wouldn't come, either," Julie said. She stood up. "Well, thank you very—" Her stiff voice choked.

"Oh, sit down. Finish your cookie," Miss Fogarty said.

Julie kept on walking toward the hallway.

"Wait—please. I'm getting used to you two. That isn't what I meant. It's just that I can't live next door to a public playground. I'd rather eat a bug!"

Ned laughed. "Then it's all right with you for Julie and me to climb the tree? But you don't want other people over there—bothering the ghost."

The woman looked startled but nodded. "That's right."

Julie couldn't tell whether she meant all of it was right.

"So that's settled. Spot up your crumbs and run along. Don't you children have homes to go to and mothers to bake cookies?"

"My mom makes cookies," Ned declared, glad to get past the awkwardness. "She can dab chocolate chip cookie dough onto the sheets faster'n you could believe."

Julie was going to let it go at that, but Miss Fogarty said, "And you? You're new here, aren't you?"

"Well, I came to live with my father. My mother is dead."

It was the first time she'd had to say it out loud since she'd moved here.

"Hey!" Ned stared at her. "You never told me."

"Ah, so that's it." The woman nodded. "You know about . . ."

Death? Sadness? Missing someone?

"I have to go now," Julie said. "Thank you very much. You coming, Ned?"

Don't pity me, she thought. Don't look at me differently.

Going along the dark hallway she stuck out her foot and tripped Ned, then squeezed his arm. "Hm, nearly fat enough to eat."

"Aw!" He shook her off.

Behind her, Julie heard Miss Fogarty's dry laugh.

Saturday Dad took Julie with him on a drive along the river to the next town, where he had some business with a man. So she didn't know whether Ned or anybody went to the tree. Some of the trees on the hills above the river showed the first washes of color change. She wondered how soon autumn color would come to the Armstrong Apartments—which rooms would be painted first with what colors.

When she told Dad that fancy, he smiled and said Jack Frost was the paint contractor.

That night, just as they were about to go to the movie, Frannie called.

"Hi, Gram! Yeah . . . yes." After talk of Frannie's doings and yes, the new jeans fit fine, the question came about making friends.

Julie said, "Well, Thursday I was climbing in a tree with two girls and a boy."

Frannie was happy about that, but Julie decided she'd better be more honest with her grandmother.

She added, "Except that one of the girls fell down the tree and isn't speaking to me."

"Oh, sweetie, don't give up. What you should do is ask her how she is and then—"

Julie listened to the advice that wasn't going to help with Sandy. "Yeah . . . uh-huh . . . . Hey, Gram, I've got to go. Dad and I were just leaving for a Charlie Chaplin movie."

She didn't say anything about Joella. Let Dad tell his mother-in-law about the skinny jogger, if he wanted to. She noticed he didn't, when he got on the phone the last few minutes.

Instead, when he hung up: "Frannie is going to drive up to see us in a couple of weeks," he reported, his voice even. "Naturally, she misses you. And she wants to see where we live."

And check up. Julie's heart gave two extra big thumps. If she couldn't show she had a busy, comfortable life here with friends, Gram would get more worried. Julie could just see the intent wrinkle that came in Frannie's forehead. She might start talking about Julie moving back "home" during Christmas vacation.

As they went out the back door to the garage, Julie did something she hadn't done for a year. She slipped her hand into Dad's and held on tight.

Monday at school Julie and Becca worked together in art period, finishing the last of the hall posters and giggling some. Sandy only looked over at them and sniffed when Becca asked her a question.

Going home on the school bus, they sat behind Julie, as usual—Sandy had commanded, "Come on, Becca"—but Sandy spent most of the time talking across the aisle to two boys, Arnold and Barry, a sixth-grader.

Julie was trying to figure out how to invite Becca to her house. What would be interesting enough to coax her? Then maybe when Frannie came, she could have Becca over, show she had a friend. She wasn't trying to eavesdrop on the conversation behind her. However, as the bus wheezed to their stop, Sandy's voice became extra loud, as if on purpose.

She said, "Last week you guys were talking about making a tree fort, you know? I can show you a good place."

7

"Where, Sandy? In your back yard?" Barry teased.

They were standing up to get off the bus.

"No, down—"

"No! Don't tell!" Julie didn't realize she had seized Sandy's hand, until Sandy pulled it away.

"I guess I can if I want to!"

Becca murmured, "Sandy, don't," as they shuffled along the aisle. "It would be—"

"Look! Whose side are you on, hers or mine?"

"My own!" Becca said. "I'm on my own side. You're always trying to boss me around."

"Hey, cat fight!" Barry exclaimed in delight.

Julie, looking back at them, stumbled on the steps,

and the bus driver said, "Watch your step! Pay attention!"

Then they were all standing on the street corner, Ned too.

Arnold said, "Now I'm curious. What's so special about this tree?"

"It's huge and perfect for a tree fort," Sandy said rapidly. "About halfway up there's a place where the branches spread."

The living room. Julie could see it boarded up, blocking the way to the top.

Ned said, "You're trying to spoil everything! Now I'm *really* sorry I didn't let you come up."

The older boys ignored him. Barry was saying, "So show us where."

"Come on." Sandy led the way downhill to the path.

Julie chewed her lip. What could she do? A tree that big couldn't be kept a secret.

"There's a reason." She tried to appeal to Arnold, but her voice whispered away.

Entering the path, the boys spotted the tree and exclaimed, "Oh, wow!" "Oh, yeah!"

Julie firmed up her voice, and then it came out too loud. "Yes, it's a wonderful tree!" she almost shouted. "But there's a good reason not to build a tree fort there. Two reasons."

"The reason being, you don't want anybody else climbing in your precious tree!" Sandy said.

"That's right!" Ned muttered.

"Maybe," Julie admitted. She had to stay brave. "What you don't know is, this land and tree belong to the city. The foreman at that factory—" She tried to explain what he'd said, according to Chester.

The boys quit listening, as they started to climb the tree.

"They could see a tree fort up there!" Julie fairly yelled. "If they did, they might forbid anybody to climb the tree!"

Barry turned around in the first crotch, and Arnold stopped on the mounting boulder.

"For sure?" Arnold asked. "Are you making this up?"

"Why should I make it up? I hate it!"

"What's the other reason?" Sandy demanded.

"I know!" Ned exclaimed. "There's an old lady next door who doesn't want a lot of people climbing around over here. She's sick and tired of it!"

Barry started climbing. "Well, pardon me for— Ooops!" He must have seen Miss Fogarty over the hedge.

Julie felt shame. The lady had asked them not to bring any more kids, and here they came with this crowd.

She tried one more thing. "They say this tree is haunted by a ghost named Gracie. Sandy, do you suppose that's why you fell? The ghost pushed you?" She saw the boys listening uneasily.

Sandy laughed, "Oh, come on!"

Barry started climbing down. "This place is too public," he said. "Boy, that old lady's got a scowl!"

Arnold stepped away from the tree. "Listen, I wouldn't want to build a fort up there, if it's going to cause a lot of trouble. A fort needs to be your own place. Sandy"—he shook his head—"you're always trying to start something." He went out to the path. "Coming, Barry?"

He was a nice kid, Julie thought. "Thank you," she ventured, but she wasn't sure he heard.

"Well!" said Sandy, watching the two boys leave. Becca went after them. " 'Bye."

Sandy turned to Julie and just looked at her for a moment. "I thought you were a scaredy-baby. But I guess you can speak up when you want to."

Right then Julie couldn't find anything to say, but Sandy went on, anyway.

"So I'll tell you what: I'll leave your tree alone, if you'll leave Becca alone. Okay?"

Julie let out a sigh and pressed her lips together. She didn't want to answer. Glancing away from Sandy, she said, "What Becca does is her own business, isn't it?" She looked back.

Sandy frowned, shrugged and whirled to run up the path. "Becca! Wait up!"

"Wuh!" Ned breathed out, flopping down on the boulder. Toward the hedge he called, "Hey, Miss

Fogarty! It wasn't our fault. Julie saved you from having a tree fort over here."

"We're leaving now," Julie called.

Then she thought she heard a chuckle.

Tuesday Julie and Ned decided to give the tree— and the old lady—a rest. Be easy, Tree, she thought, as she walked by, and leaves on the elbow-branch waved at her. Going close to the hedge, she called, "Miss Fogarty?" but there was no reply.

That evening she and Dad watched TV. The Charlie Chaplin movie had been a lot better. She'd laughed and laughed, along with Dad and Joella, who sat on the other side of Dad. Afterward, Joella had taken them to a place she said made breaded pork tenderloins the "good old-fashioned way." Julie had to admit it was the best one she'd ever eaten.

Joella was coming over Friday night to make white spaghetti for them. So what? All spaghetti was white. And Dad could make spaghetti, anyway. It was like the beginning of the end, like launching down the tallest slide on the playground. Yet at the fish fry Dad had talked a long time to a young woman from his office.

Oh—she couldn't wear herself out, wondering, Is this one going to be my stepmother? Is that the one? Anyone?

She had more immediate things to worry about. In less than two weeks Frannie would be here. And she'd made no progress at making friends, unless Gram would count Ned. On the bus that day Becca had sat with Sandy, as usual, and had said only, "Hi," waggling her fingers at Julie. Sandy had nothing to say to her. The poster project was finished, so there was no chance to talk to Becca much at school.

Julie waited until the commercial. "Dad?"

"Wha—" He came unglued from the screen.

"Listen. If Gram thinks I'm not adjusting here, will you let her make me go back?"

The TV set chattered on about auto sales, and she wished she could turn it off. It wasn't right to have to discuss such important things during the commercial.

Dad said, "Your grandmother just wants to see you. She just wants what's best for you." His eyes went back to the screen.

"Oh, come on, Dad! That's a cop-out! Is that what *you* think? That it's better I go back there?"

He got up and clicked off the TV set. "No. I want you here. You belong with me."

She knew he meant it. But . . . Mom used to say Frannie could talk the leg off a chair. Julie gripped her fingers together. "Will you tell her that?"

"Yes. But"—he sighed, picking up his recorder

from the end table—"it's hard for Frannie, missing you. She loves you, too, and we both have to decide what's really best for you."

"*I* know what's best for me!" Julie said in a burst. "To be here with you."

"Huh!" Dad snorted. "You're getting to sound as strong-minded as your grandmother." He smiled. "Listen, you tell her what you've told me about the kids and the tree and the old lady. She'll see you're involved with more people than you ever were back there."

"Oh!" She hadn't thought about it that way. She wasn't sure any of those people thought of her as a friend. Well, probably Ned did. Dared she take Frannie to meet Miss Fogarty? Julie tried to picture the old lady getting out the painted china and serving tea. *Huh*, she snorted in turn. Probably not. But she could take Gram to see the tree, and maybe they would talk to Miss Fogarty over the back fence.

"Okay, I'll tell Frannie," she said to Dad, who had started *pooting* lovely notes out of the recorder. "I have to do some homework now."

She went to the kitchen table and spread out maps. Music sounded from the living room, as Dad played the recorder. She liked to hear him in there playing while she worked.

After the last note there was a silence in the living room. She got up to see. He was just sitting there, looking off into space. She went over and hugged him, and he hugged her, too.

The next afternoon, while Ned was busy with Scouts, Julie said, "Hello, Tree," and climbed it. She wanted to think about what had happened that afternoon. Where would be the best thinking spot? Not the tower, with all the world spread out for her to look at. The side attic, she decided. It was high, yet other branches above and around made it a sheltered place for thinking.

As she settled on the limb with her feet steadied on the one below, she recognized this was the same place she'd worried about the ghost of Gracie. She wasn't going to do that now. Still, the memory made her look at the house next door. No eyes watching her from the upper window, and no little woman in the back yard.

This afternoon, just before school was out, she and Becca had been in the restroom, no one else around. While they washed their hands, Becca had said, "Say, Julie, listen. I'll tell you a secret, if you'll tell me one first." Becca had smiled teasingly at her in the mirror above the wash basins.

Secrets! Julie had gotten excited. Becca was offering her a secret. She'd thought fast, what to tell? That she believed in fairies? No, not that. What did she have that was special to offer?

She remembered hearing her voice shake as she'd

begun, "Um, you know about my mother." Becca nodded, face sympathetic. That had come out through their teacher, when Sandy was lining up mothers to drive them to the circus train.

"Well, the secret is," she'd confessed, "I might be getting a stepmother, and I'm scared of it." Right away she knew it was too clumsy, too heavy.

"Oh." Becca had sounded disappointed but added, "Don't be scared. Sandy's got a stepmother and a stepfather, both, and she gets along with them fine."

That was different. It meant Sandy had a real mother. "Don't tell Sandy!" she'd begged.

Becca had promised, "No, a secret is a secret. Okay, now listen." She'd grinned. "Mr. Armbruster wears a wig."

Julie had noticed her startled face in the mirror. *That* was the secret? Their teacher, big burly Mr. Armbruster, wore a wig?

Early one morning, Becca had gone on to tell, she'd looked out her bedroom window, when Mr. Armbruster came jogging down the street. And the top of his head was bald. "He didn't have his hair on," she'd said, giggling. "Not on top. He's got lots on his legs."

Then Julie did laugh. "Oh, Becca, you're so funny."

Of course, going back to the room, she had stared at the teacher, but she couldn't tell which part of his sandy hair was real.

Thinking it over now, though, she wished she

hadn't told that secret. Becca had hardly seemed to care. Could she trust Becca? Would Becca accidentally blurt it out to Sandy someday? And what was it she didn't want Sandy to know? The part that she was *scared* of getting a stepmother. Sandy was tough, and she didn't want that girl to know she was scared.

The thing about Mr. Armbruster seemed so silly in comparison. Still, it could be something they could share and laugh about. At least, Becca had offered it.

Whush—something bounced the branch her feet were resting on. Not the crow again! Instead, it was Squirrel, running along the limb with a nut in his mouth. Her feet were on his runway from the pear tree. The squirrel stopped.

Julie held on to a nearby branch and pulled up her feet. *Go on*, she willed. She didn't say it, not to scare the squirrel. The white rings of his eyes flicked up at her, then he ran on. She watched his tail disappear into the hollow, and his head popped right out of the hole again, nut deposited. She kept her feet up, as the squirrel ran back along the branch without an upward glance.

"Oh, Squirrel," Julie chuckled, as he flew over to the pear tree. She wondered how far he had to go to find nuts and how soon he'd be back. She certainly couldn't do much thinking with a squirrel running back and forth under her feet. Come to think of it, maybe she was done thinking for now. Smiling, Julie climbed down.

As she crossed the street, the teenager, Chester, came out of the factory with a box and dumped a shower of dust and metal things into an oil drum. As soon as he went back inside, Julie hurried to the trash barrel and peered down. Immediately he popped his head out of the door again. Just like Squirrel.

"What are you doing?"

"I was wondering—looking for—I've never seen a turkey bit."

"Then how do you know what you're looking for?"

He was going to be mean. She started to walk on.

No, he wasn't. "If you want to see turkey bits, come on in." He opened the door wider.

Should she? She went in.

Swaggering a little, Chester led the way to a machine that was going *clack-clack-ti-clack-clack*, loud and clear.

"We make all kinds of rings," he said, as if he owned the place. "Hog rings, rings to clamp upholstery on frames, rings to put up fences. But this machine, right now it's making turkey rings—turkey bits."

Machines had always been a mystery to Julie; but this black greasy one had so many moving parts doing different things it looked funny. At the top it ate in copper wire, and after all that commotion, at the bottom it spit out little pieces. Julie laughed.

"It's not funny," Chester said severely. "See this center forming post?" he pointed. "See those slides moving back and forth? They come in and cut the wire and shape it, and the bits fall in that box."

He picked one out of the box. It was a small C with a half-inch opening between the slanted ends.

"But what is it for?" She was still mystified.

"To keep turkeys from pecking, dummy. See, when they're raised in big flocks, they don't have enough room of their own, so they try to peck each other to death."

How gruesome. Julie's shoulders shuddered. She thought of the turkey breast from a box that Dad had heated up for dinner last Sunday.

"The bit goes between the turkey's jaws, and he can eat, but he can't completely close his beak. See, they put the ends in his nose holes and clamp it with pliers, so the bit hangs down in his mouth. Like this."

With pliers Chester squeezed the ends closer together and hooked the turkey bit on her nose.

"Hey, don't!"

The C dangled from the narrow part of her nostrils, and the boy guffawed. "You look like a turkey, all right!"

Julie unhooked the copper ring. It hadn't hurt.

She should have known he'd pull some kind of trick on her. But it gave her an idea.

"Could I have this?"

"Naw. That part down there counts exactly a hundred to a box. Don't want to short nobody."

He reached to take it from her, but a man said, "Let her have it."

"Oh! Well, sure, Mr. Potter. I was just show-ing—"

Julie saw a short round man who must be the owner. Holding the turkey bit, she said, "Thank you. Sir." Probably she shouldn't be here. "Uh, that's an interesting machine. Did you make it?"

He looked pleased. "No, but my great-grandfather designed it." He looked over his glasses at her. "Hm. You're the girl in the tree."

She *had* been seen. He must have watched her, to recognize her now. Julie nodded unhappily.

"I told her," Chester started, but the man ignored him, saying, "What does Miss Fogarty think of you and that boy climbing the tree?"

"Not much," Julie admitted. Was he going to tell her not to climb it?

But he said only, "Yes, she keeps to herself. I've been in the factory since I was a boy, yet I've never been in her house."

"I have."

He'd been turning away, but he looked back at her. "Well! You must be special."

Even so, seeing the way he hurried off, she thought she'd better get out of his workplace. "Well, thank you very much," she told Chester. "It's been very interesting, but I have to go home now." She started toward the door.

"You're welcome," he said, being as formal as she. Then, "Hey, kid?"

He looked as if he didn't know what to do with his face. The grimace of a grin slid off his mouth leaving his eyes—were they looking sorry? She thought he was going to apologize for the times he'd acted mean.

Instead, he said, "You better play in that tree while you can. I been hearing things."

"What?" Julie exclaimed. "What?"

"Aw, I don't know—maybe nothing." He turned to his push broom.

"Tell me! You're teasing me again, aren't you?"

"No. Ask the city guys."

8

At supper Julie told her father what Chester had said. And that night in her gable room she dreamed she was racing Joella to the tree. She climbed it ahead of Joella, but the higher she got, the more tangled she became in tree branches. Then Joella was shrinking, and Julie was leading her up the tree like a mother.

Somehow she felt better at breakfast, especially when Dad said he'd try to find out if anything was happening about the vacant land and the tree. Possibly Chester was only trying to torment her.

She took the turkey bit with her, and when Ned got to the bus stop, she put it in her nose.

"You know what this is?" she said with some difficulty. The circle dangled and bumped her upper lip.

"Piece of wire hanging out of your nose. What's the matter with you?"

"It's a turkey bit!" She laughed. "You know, when they harness a turkey and ride it!"

"Aww. Let me see." Ned tried it in his nose, but it fell out.

Julie put it back in her nostrils. "Gobble, gobble!"

"She's gone crazy!" exclaimed Sandy, who had just walked up. "What is that thing?"

"It's a turkey bit from Potter's factory." When she said *Potter's*, her lip blew the ring off, but she caught it. So Sandy was talking to her again.

Sandy laughed. "I always knew you were a turkey."

"They put them in turkeys' beaks to keep them from pecking each other to death." Julie gave Sandy back a stare. "Maybe we all should wear turkey bits."

"Oh yeah?" Sandy looked at her. "You think I should muffle my beak? Hey"—her voice eased— "let's not fight. You mind if I try it?"

Julie carefully wiped the ends that had been in her nose and handed it to Sandy, as the bus came. "Don't let it fall off."

Arnold, getting on behind Sandy, saw her wearing the thing. "Look where the girls are wearing their earrings now!"

"It's a turkey bit, gobble, gobble," Sandy clowned.

94

"Really, it's Julie's. She got it from that factory down there." Handing it back, she whispered, "I dare you to put it on in class."

So Julie did. And Mr. Armbruster never noticed what the kids were laughing at. When Julie put the C-ring in her jeans pocket, she couldn't help feeling grateful to Chester and Mr. Potter.

Morning clouds cleared to a sunny afternoon, so Julie and Ned went down the hill to Wilder-land. As they started on the path, Ned was saying, "Do you suppose Chester would give me a turkey bit?" He stopped. "Uh-oh."

There were two men in the vacant lot, and they had surveying instruments. The one near the sidewalk across from the factory stood at a tripod bearing a transit; the other with the line was just beyond the tree. Julie and Ned ran toward them.

"That do it?" shouted the man with the line. The two men approached each other, the one winding up his metal tape. "That tree will have to come out," he said.

"Too bad. Old monster," said the other, glancing up at the mulberry tree. "Be a job to get the roots out."

"What?" Julie screamed. "What are you doing?"

The men looked at her in surprise. "Surveying," said the tripod engineer. "City's going to put in a big parking lot here."

Clack, said the factory, but she couldn't *not* hear the words. *Parking lot*. Her face felt cold and stiff. "No," she made her lips move. "You can't. Not the tree."

"Hey now, missy. What's the matter?"

"She loves that tree!" Ned blurted. "So do I. And the old lady next door—lots of people! You can't make a parking lot here."

"It can't happen." Julie shook her head.

"Look, don't start trouble," said the lineman. "We're just doing our jobs."

"I'm sorry," said the other. "Sure, it's a good old tree. But the City Council voted for the parking lot. It was in last night's paper."

Julie never read the newspaper. "It can't happen," she repeated.

"Sorry, kids." He did look sorry. "But there's lots more trees in Sutterville. You can find another one." The two men started toward the street.

Ned called after them, "When? The tree—when will they cut it down?"

"I don't know." The engineer folded up his tripod. "Sometime next week, probably." He put the instruments in a city car at the curb.

It was Ned who cried, not Julie. "No-o!" He threw himself down and pulled at fistfuls of grass. "I hate this!" He began to sob.

Julie stood in shock, watching the men drive away. Her throat was so tight and full, she could hardly breathe. At last she pulled in a big breath. "Ned, come on. We've got to find Miss Fogarty."

"Yeah!" He got up, wiping wet smudges on his cheeks. "Don't tell anybody I—"

Julie was already running to the alley and around to push open the wire gate. "Miss Fogarty!" she yelled.

The back yard was the same as it had been for two days, deserted. Ned looked in the shed. "Nobody in there, not even the cat."

They knocked at the back door, rattled the screen, which was latched. They raced around to the front and rang the bell. No little woman came.

"Why does she have to be gone, just when we need her?" Julie cried.

"Maybe she isn't," Ned said in a small voice. "What if she's dead inside there?"

"Oh, no!" Julie exclaimed angrily. "Don't even think that!"

"Maybe we better try to find out," he insisted.

He turned the doorknob, but it was locked, and so was the window on the front porch. Then they found the kitchen window open a wide crack. Julie tried to push it up, but it wouldn't move.

"It's wedged inside somehow."

Looking through the window, they saw Puss curled up on a throw rug, one paw pulled around her head.

"Puss, where is she?" Julie said. "Miss Fogarty!" she called in.

The cat opened one blue eye and closed it again. Near the back door was a bowl containing some dry cat food and a bowl of water.

"She's not in there dead!" Julie declared. "She's gone somewhere."

"I guess so," Ned agreed. "She fixed the window open, so Puss can go in and out. But why did she go away? What should we do?" he begged.

"I don't know." Julie's eyes were beginning to prickle. "Ned, I don't know." She saw tears in his eyes, too, and touched one of his knobby shoulders. "Ned, let's go home now. Let's ask our parents, and I'll think—" She gulped at the choking in her throat. "You think. 'Bye."

As she walked away, she couldn't bear to look at the tree.

At home it was too awful to think about. Julie made herself comfortable on her bed and began to read a fairy tale book. The story was about a woodcutter. She flung down the book, wailing, "No-o!"

They couldn't cut down the tree. She heard the chain saw ripping, saw the enormous tree toppled on the ground, boughs cut off. Horrible torn hole in the earth . . . "No-o!"

Dad came in through the kitchen, and this time she didn't wait for him to come up and find her crying. She rushed downstairs and tried to tell him in a burst of sobs, ". . . cut down the tree! . . . parking lot out of Wilder-land!"

He crouched and gathered her in his arms. "I know, Julie, I know." He smoothed the hair away from her face. "I called the city offices today and found out."

"So what are we going to do?" she demanded, sobbing.

"I don't know. The council voted and work starts next week."

He was always so reasonable. And he never solved anything. Always saying *I don't know*. Julie kicked his leg.

He only held her closer. "Julie, don't. Don't hurt yourself so."

"Ohh!" she wailed. "And Miss Fogarty is gone, just when we need her. She's the only grown-up who cares about that tree!"

"Well, I do, too. It's a wonderful tree. Look"— he led her to sit on the living-room couch—"Julie, that walnut tree out in back—I could nail a ladder of steps on it, and that could be your tree."

"No! It wouldn't be the same. Ned comes to the mulberry tree, and the old elf lady is there, and there's a ghost in the tree!"

"Ghost?"

"Oh, Dad—" She didn't feel like explaining. She hid her face against his shoulder and rested there.

"I'm sorry. I'm sorry about it all." He smoothed

99

her hair. "Now, in the meantime, we need to eat. Let's go out and eat pork tenderloins."

Julie squirmed in protest against his jacket. She didn't want to go out and eat in public, where she couldn't cry.

But she did. She forced down the first cardboard bite, and after she got to chewing the tenderloin sandwich, it tasted almost as good as the first time.

That night in bed she thought about the walnut tree in the back yard, trying to remember whether there were decent branches to sit on. It could be a private place.

"But it's not the same," she muttered.

This time she heard herself. By now part of loving the mulberry tree was tied up with people. She'd wanted it for her own place, hadn't wanted to share it with Ned. My tree! she had thought. Yet it had become special because of the people, too. Even having Silly-Billy and Becca there had been fun.

"Ohh!" She thrashed over to her other side. She was too tired to start worrying and crying again. She let her mind slide away into sleep.

In the morning she knew there could be no more sliding away from it. They must not cut down the tree. What could she do to stop them?

Ned ran up to the bus stop. "My mom was no help, and Dad's gone away on a job. Have you thought of something?"

"I'm thinking."

All through the morning classes she tried to think. At breakfast she'd asked Dad who he had talked to at the city offices and what the person had actually said. He'd spoken with the Director of Public Works, Frank Bailey, who said they would start getting the land ready next week. They'd need to bulldoze back into the hill.

This was Friday. What if they sneaked in this morning and cut down the tree? She should have stayed there.

What could stop them? She could call the man and beg him to at least leave the tree there, but she didn't think it would do any good. What could make the tree special to other people, so they'd want to keep it?

If it was an historic tree the Indians signed a treaty under, they'd keep it. What if it was actually the oldest, biggest mulberry tree in Sutterville—or even the last mulberry tree?

At lunch hour she got permission to use the telephone in the school office and called the Department of Public Works. Mr. Bailey was out to lunch, she was told.

"Oh, well, uh"—her voice got smaller—"who's in charge of him?"

"The City Manager. He's out to lunch, too. Little girl, is this some kind of joke?"

"It's no joke. Thank you. Good-bye."

In the cafeteria she found Ned. "Come on," she said, and went over to the table where Becca and Sandy were sitting.

She said, "Listen, you know that tree we climbed in? Do you care anything about that tree?"

Becca smiled, "Sure, let's—"

"I care enough to want to climb it again," Sandy said, "and show that tree it can't throw me on the ground!"

"The city wants a big parking lot there. Next week they are going to cut down the tree. Do you want to help?"

"Oh, Julie, how terrible!" Becca exclaimed.

Sandy said, "Help what? Cut it down?"

Julie felt like hitting her, and Ned said, "Aw, nuts," turning away from the girls.

"No! Do you want to help stop them?"

Sandy nodded with a mocking smile. "Sure, stop the city. How do you think kids could do that?"

Ned looked at Julie hopefully as she began. "We could make signs that say Don't Kill Me and Save This Tree and Oldest Tree in Sutterville and hang them on the tree." She saw the doubt on Sandy's face and hurried on, "And we could all go sit in the tree so they couldn't cut it down." She knew Sandy would like that action part.

"Hm," Sandy considered, "a tree sit-in. Maybe the newspaper would come and take pictures."

"Hey!" Ned said. "We'll guard the tree. If one of us is sitting in it all the time—"

"Becca," Julie appealed, "you're good at making posters."

"Sure, let's do it!" Sandy decided. "It probably won't stop them, but that's a good old tree, and it's worth a try. And it'll be fun. We'll need more help." She began to take charge. "I'll get Arnold and Barry. Julie, you call the newspaper."

Julie didn't mind. She'd actually persuaded Sandy! Ned added to her glow by telling her what a great idea it was and offering to bring Silly-Billy.

"The oldest tree in Sutterville, my!" Becca marveled. "When do we make the posters and signs?"

Julie knew she'd have to verify that about the tree, but she let it go for now. "In art class and recess, if Mr. Armbruster will let us."

"Yeah, well, when's the tree sit-in?" Sandy asked. "When are they going to come for that tree?"

"That's what I'm trying to find out. Maybe we'll do it Monday."

"Good, because I can't until then. We're going away for the weekend."

From there on, things began to fizzle out. Mr. Armbruster wouldn't let them use school materials or time for the posters, "After the flack I caught about that circus outing." Becca wanted to know how they could guard the tree all day, when they had to be in school. And when Julie phoned the Department of Public Works during afternoon recess, both men were out.

The lady on the phone admitted, "They're scheduled to start work on the parking lot Tuesday morning."

Coming away from the phone, Julie bumped into the school secretary, because she could hardly see. To have the day of your death named! Tuesday. Thank goodness, the tree couldn't know.

After school when Julie and Ned hurried down the hill, Wilder-land was deserted, and the tree stood there, same as always. Another thank goodness! Julie put her arms around the trunk as far as she could and laid her cheek against the bark.

"Oh, stop that mushy stuff," Ned said, wiping his nose. "Let's go see if she's back."

Miss Fogarty wasn't. The cat was in the yard, and her bowls, when they looked in the kitchen window, were nearly empty.

Going back to the tree, they climbed with familiar ease to the top. Julie saw other treetops were flecked with brilliant reds and yellows. Ned took a look, while she wedged in the branches just below.

They planned. That night they'd make posters with whatever they could find at home. First thing in the morning they would meet at the tree and hang the signs on it. Becca had promised to bring signs, too, but she wouldn't be able to stay, because she had a dance class. Ned would guard the tree, while Julie went to the Tree and Seed Company to try to find out whether this one really was the oldest or the only mulberry tree in Sutterville. After that she'd stop at the newspaper to tell what they were doing for the tree.

Ned kept saying, "Yeah! Wow! It's gonna be great!" But the more she heard herself naming those things out loud, the more uneasy Julie felt.

The town clock struck five, and they decided the tree was safe for the night. Leaving, Julie saw Chester come out of Potter's factory.

"You knew," she said. "About the parking lot and the tree."

He got on his motorcycle, but he didn't start the racket. "Yeah. Tough."

"Well, we're going to do something about it! We're going to save the tree!" She told him the plans.

"You silly kids." He shook his head. "It won't work." Then the racket began.

Julie was afraid he was right.

When Julie got home, Joella was in the kitchen chopping vegetables. "Hi!" she called. "I'm starting the spaghetti."

In all the real troubles Julie had forgotten about that. Dad came in the back way with a sack of groceries. Julie ignored Joella.

"Dad, listen!" She told him the plans to save the

tree. Knowing how weak they sounded, she tried to pump it up. "Everybody in town will know!"

She wasn't surprised when he shook his head. "Oh, Julie, I'm sorry. I'm afraid the city officials won't pay any attention. They will have to take the tree out to get their big square parking lot."

"But the tree could make shade for some of the cars."

"And drop mulberries on them. Julie, honey—"

"Hey, she's got a right to try, hasn't she?" Joella said.

Julie's head swiveled to look at the young woman. What was she trying to do?

"There's no point to it," Dad said. "It won't work."

"How do you know? Anyway, if I loved a tree, I'd want to try to save its life."

"I don't want her to get hurt."

"She's hurt already."

Julie watched this exchange with interest. When Mom and Dad used to argue about her, their voices got louder and louder.

Dad said firmly, "I want Julie to face reality. Look, honey, what do you expect the sit-in to accomplish? Do you think the city will give up a parking lot to save a tree?"

"That's a good point," Joella put in. "When you demonstrate, you have to know what you're asking for, what you want."

Now they were united in tormenting her. "No!"

she spat out. "I guess grown-ups wouldn't give up a parking lot just for a tree!"

Then what could she hope for? What she wanted was to keep the tree alive.

"All right," she said, "this is what the sit-in is asking for: that they leave the part the tree is on and where Gracie's house was."

"Good! Now you're cooking," Joella approved. "Who's Gracie?"

"Leave a strip of land," Dad said thoughtfully. "Like a strip park?"

"Oh!" A public park.

"Speaking of cooking, did you get the baby clams?" Joella asked Dad.

"Here." He took two cans from the grocery sack and opened them. "Shall I dump them in the sauce?"

Julie looked in the pot on the stove. It contained a creamy white sauce. "Yuck! Clams? Where's the burger and the tomato sauce?"

"This is why it's called *white* spaghetti." Joella smiled. "Vegetarian, except for the clams. Very healthy and, I promise, very good."

"Oh. Well. Excuse me." Julie went down to the basement to hunt for poster materials.

A public park. People eating sack lunches at a picnic table. No longer a wonderful magical private tree. They might hang a swing on it. Miss Fogarty would hate it, might even move away.

So, let them cut down the tree rather than share

it? No! It was her first friend here. Now it was her turn to be the tree's friend.

Julie came upstairs with a cardboard carton. "This is all I can find that's stiff enough to make posters. May I borrow your knife," she asked Joella, "to cut it up?"

Joella handed the knife to her, then said, "I think I have some poster board left over from when we demonstrated for women's rights. I'll run home and see, if you'll chop these carrots." From the door she called back, "Have you thought about a petition? Asking people to sign a petition to save the tree?"

Chopping, while Dad stirred the sauce, Julie wondered about Joella. Maybe the woman was trying to make up to her, but she was nice to try to help. And she and Ned needed every bit of help they could get. How should she word her poster? "We want Mulberry Park"? No, let's see, Julie figured. She felt too nervous to eat some strange new spaghetti.

9

DON'T KILL ME, read the sign that swung in the early-morning breeze. Listening to the whisper of leaves, Julie wished Ned would get there. She went down for the next sign, OLD HISTORIC TREE, and climbed higher to find a place where it could be seen from the street.

"*Now* what are you doing to that tree?" The squawk was Miss Fogarty's voice. She hurried from the alley. "I couldn't read—'Don't Kill Me'— What on earth?"

"Oh, Miss Fogarty!" Hastily Julie hooked the sign on a branch and climbed down. "You're back! Oh, why did you go away, just when we needed you?"

"Had to get away from all the hullabaloo next door. Took the bus to St. Louis to see my sister.

Boring woman. Now what's all this about?" She stood with her hands on her hips, looking up at OLD HISTORIC TREE swaying in the breeze.

"Parking lot . . . next Tuesday . . . in the paper," Julie babbled.

"I stopped the paper while I was away. Here, slow down and tell me straight."

Julie did her best, starting with the surveyors. She told about the town's plan for a parking lot. "And the lady at the office said they'll start work Tuesday."

"Lord help us!" Miss Fogarty flopped down on the mounting rock. "A parking lot right up to my hedge! And Gracie's tree? Gone?"

"No! We're going to save the tree! That's why the signs." Julie explained the plan for the tree sit-in.

"Pshaw! You think the city will stop for a bunch of kids perched in a tree? Oh, Lord have mercy!"

"If we can get enough people to care, sign a petition to save the tree, maybe the city would stop. I mean," she had to put this idea carefully, "stop short of the tree. Let it stand on its strip of land next to your house. They could have a parking lot and the rest could be—"

"Hm, yes." Miss Fogarty started to nod. "Maybe—"

"—like a little park," Julie finished in a small voice.

The old lady's head jerked. "Park? No!"

Julie touched one of her hands. "I know. People

come to parks. But we can't let them cut down the tree, can we?"

Miss Fogarty smacked a hand against her thigh. "No! But"—she gave Julie a sharp look—"what if nobody else cares? Sutterville's full of trees. A petition with five names—pshaw!"

"Maybe we could get the city people to care," Julie insisted. "I tried to call Mr. Bailey, the Director of Public Works, but he wasn't there. I'm going to call his home today. And if—"

"Little Frankie Bailey! I've known him since he started pushing a shovel for the Street Department. Never you mind calling him." Miss Fogarty sprang up so full of energy, Julie could almost see sparks shooting out of her. "I'll give him a piece of my mind! Right now!" She trotted toward the alley.

It was going as Julie had secretly hoped. Miss Fogarty had worked for the city for years. Maybe she could stop them. Julie started after her to hear what happened, but Becca arrived just then with her poster.

She ran from the street, where her mother waited in a car, and her poster was magnificent. As she ran, it flashed and rippled with streamers. The words read simply, SAVE THIS TREE, but Becca had used orange glow paint for the letters and sprinkled them with sparkles.

"This is all I could get done," she gasped. "I've got to hurry, 'cause we're late."

"Oh, but Becca, it's wonderful, terrific!" Julie exclaimed, and Becca smiled at the praise. "Listen, there's more hope! Miss Fogarty is calling the man in charge right now to tell him he can't cut down the tree!"

"Oh, how marvelous! Call me tonight and let me know!" Becca dashed back to the car.

Julie started again for the alley, when Ned called from the path, "Sorry I'm late." Running, he sailed his poster out behind him on a long cord, like a kite.

"Ned! It's so—" Julie couldn't find the words.

Ned had taken the direct approach. Staring out of white paint was a large black skull and crossbones. Underneath, big black letters read, DEATH TO ANYONE WHO HURTS THIS TREE!!

"I don't know." Julie worried about the threat. "It looks scary."

"Sure, it is! We need to scare them. Here, help me get this up the tree, where it'll show. Hey." He stopped to admire Becca's poster. "That's great. We'll get that up, too."

They had an awkward time of it, lifting the posters between boughs and getting them to hang from branches that stuck out to face the street. While they worked, Julie told Ned about Miss Fogarty ("Back? Yow! Great!") and the phone call she was making ("Fantastic! Wait till he sees this!")

They had the hardest time with Julie's long sign, LET ME LIVE, because she wanted it to stream out like a banner above the top branches. Although they tied it on as high as they dared to go, when they climbed down and looked, the words were partly hidden by leaves. However, the bright colors did make the tree look as if it were wearing a crown. In fact, the whole tree looked amazing, studded with signs.

"What will poor Squirrel think?" Julie murmured. One poster hung from his runway.

"Huh! Poor Squirrel won't have a tree to live in, if— Hey, there she is!"

As Miss Fogarty came from the alley, they hurried to meet her, and Julie stopped smiling when she heard the woman's grumbling tone.

"—lackadaisical fools to run Sutterville. He's gone for the weekend to a football game. City Manager, too. No wonder this town is going to rack and ruin. Fine old library torn down to make room for a shopping mall, and now this!"

"You didn't talk to him." Julie's voice thudded.

"No, silly! That's what I just told you. And that's not true," she said, pointing to OLD HISTORIC TREE fluttering in the breezes. "Nothing historic about this tree—poor thing, all decked out like a Christmas tree," she fussed.

"But could it be the only mulberry tree in town?" Julie begged.

"No. Mulberry trees were popular, back a while. However"—Miss Fogarty cocked her head to study

OLDEST TREE IN SUTTERVILLE—"that could be true. It's anybody's guess which tree is the oldest. Until they cut it down and count the rings."

"Oh, Miss Fogarty!" Julie wailed.

"Hey, are you giving up?" Ned demanded of the woman.

"Of course not!" She stalked around the tree to see the other posters. "I'm just mad. Mad as a wet cat!" And frustrated, she said, because she would have to wait until Monday to talk to "that Frankie."

While there was hope, Julie had thought they might not need to hold the tree sit-in. Now they'd have to go ahead with the plans. There was the other part she hadn't told Ned.

"Look," she said, "it would be good if we could get people to sign a petition. But we'll have to spell out what we're asking for."

"Save the tree!" Ned declared.

"But if they won't pay attention to Miss Fogarty, if they won't give up having a big parking lot . . ." Julie explained what she'd been thinking, while the old lady listened, her face grim. "Maybe we should ask for a park, just the land the tree is on, from the alley out to the street."

"Park!" he yelled. "Everybody coming here!"

"Hmph!" Miss Fogarty marched back to her house.

"I know. But we better ask for something we might get."

Julie left Ned to think about it and guard the tree, while she went to the newspaper office to tell about the demonstration. *All those kids and signs in the tree should make a good picture.* She rehearsed how she would try to talk to the grown-up strangers. From the street Ned's and Becca's posters showed up well; but none of the people in the passing cars even glanced toward the tree.

When Julie trudged back from downtown, it was mid-morning and Ned lay stretched out in the grass under the tree. "So?" He sat up.

She shook her head. "The Tree Company people didn't know anything about our tree, and there was hardly anybody in the newspaper office. The girl at the desk was nice, though. She said she'd tell the City Editor, when he came back." Actually, Julie suspected the girl had been trying not to laugh at her.

"Call him on the phone Monday, that's the way," Ned said. "Uh, I been thinking. I guess if Griselda"—he looked toward the hedge—"if Miss Fogarty can't stop the city, can't save all of Wilder-land—well, yeah, we ought to ask them to make a park of this piece. Anything to save the tree."

"Yes." Julie smiled at him. If they cut it down, would she and Ned stop being friends? She hoped not.

He said he'd promised his mom to come back and

do his Saturday chores, and Julie said she would stay until noon, just in case workers came.

"If I see anybody with a chain saw, I'll climb to the top and refuse to come down!" she vowed.

"Thattaway, Julie!" he cheered, running to the path.

Meantime she sat on the rock.

"No help at the daily paper?" Whenever Miss Fogarty's voice came through the hedge, it seemed to grate more witchily. Had she heard Ned call her Griselda?

"Not much." Julie walked around to the alley gate to talk to her. The woman had on garden gloves, cutting back daisies. "But, Miss Fogarty? What are you going to say, when you talk to Mr. Bailey? What if he won't listen to you? Would you tie yourself to the tree?"

"Hah!" Her voice still grated, as she crouched at a drooping daisy clump. "Not me—crazy old lady getting her picture in the paper." She stood up and looked at Julie, her eyes perking. "Now this is what. You stop worrying about that tree. I'm going to give this whole parking lot plan a lot of thought over the weekend." She bent over the daisies again.

Weekend. "The weekend after this one my grandmother is coming," Julie said. "I wanted to show her the tree. What if it's gone!"

"Stop that!"

"Well, uh, I wish Frannie could meet you, too."

Miss Fogarty gave her a sharp look. "Why?"

"Oh, if you don't want to. It's just she'd like to meet my—the people I know. If she thinks I'm not making friends here, maybe she'll want me to go back and live with her."

There. She'd already told more than she meant to.

Clicking her shears, Miss Fogarty attacked some tall blue delphinium that had fallen over. "So? Is she so bad to you? The wicked fairy?" The woman smiled at the fallen stalks.

"No!" Julie protested. "She's good. But I want to live with my father. Say, you've never met Dad, either. He's—special. He plays the recorder and loves tree-climbing and—"

"Merciful heavens! I know enough people already." She glanced up at Julie. "But, yes, child, bring your grandmother around."

The back yard grayed as the sun went under a cloud. "Oh, I hope it doesn't rain on our signs!" Julie looked at them waving in the tree, strange decorations.

Miss Fogarty eyed the sky. "Not going to rain."

"And oh, what if they come Monday instead of Tuesday? What if they cut down the tree, while we're in school?" Her voice cracked with the strain of it all.

"I'll keep an eye on that tree." Miss Fogarty stood up, pulling off her gloves. "Now you stop worrying about this, that and the other. Go home and play or read or something. I need to think about this tree business."

"All right." Julie went home.

The next afternoon Julie climbed in the Armstrong Apartments by herself. She wanted one more time alone with the tree—in case. On the way up she straightened two posters the wind had skewed against branches, and she hung a poster Joella had made. It read GIVE US MULBERRY PARK.

Joella had come to the house with it that morning and stayed awhile to help Julie figure out the wording for the petition. They decided on, *We oppose cutting down the fine old mulberry tree near Fourth and Jefferson Streets to make way for a parking lot. Leave the tree on its strip of land for a small park.*

"You'll need somebody to get the signatures," Joella had said. "I'd offer to do it, but I don't get off work until five."

"I'll do it," Dad volunteered. "The computer world can wait. I wouldn't miss this tree sit-in for anything!"

It felt good to have Dad and Joella caring and helping. Julie thought that in accepting Joella's help it was kind of like accepting Joella as okay. But— why not?

Swaying a little in the top branches, she looked out toward the spire of St. Mark's Church and the maple tree flaming rosy below the spire. Maybe some Sunday she and Dad could go to Miss Fogarty's church.

She noticed some extra color near her banner. On one twig the leaves had turned yellow. So the tree's autumn glory had started. By Halloween the tree might be a ball of gold.

However, she suddenly knew, she would not come here on Halloween night, looking for the ghost of Gracie Wolcott. It would be disrespectful, as if Gracie could be a funny made-up ghost in costume, popping out on cue.

And the tree might not even be here, come Halloween. . . . Don't even think it!

Still, she made a point of sitting in each of her favorite places before she climbed down.

Miss Fogarty came out of the alley, saying, "Here, help me measure." She handed Julie a carpenter's tape. "Stand over there by the hedge and hold the case. I need to find out how much land we're asking for."

She walked off, unreeling the yellow metal tape, until she was well past the bushing-out of tree branches. "Yes, twenty feet," she called. "Walk here, so the tape goes back in."

When Julie got up to her, tape recoiled, Miss Fogarty said, "I happen to know they can't build within five feet of a property line. Want to make sure they don't hurt the roots, when they dig down."

Julie looked at the rest of Wilder-land and imagined it flat, paved over, growing nothing but parking meters. Such a small space left for the tree to stand on, for a park.

Still, the fact that the old lady was measuring must mean she'd made up her mind to the idea of a park next door.

"You think of everything," Julie said.

"Hmph. Not quite. Just want to have my figures right, when I talk to Frankie Bailey tomorrow."

Then Monday afternoon everybody was finding his or her best place to perch in the tree.

Sandy ran down the path first, followed by Barry and Arnold, who shouted, "Hey! Hey! Save the tree!" And, "Awesome!" when they caught sight of Ned's skull and crossbones. Ned wasn't there to hear the praise, because he had gone home to fetch Silly-Billy.

"I bet Julie made all the rest of the posters," Sandy said to another girl who rode the bus, Tanya.

"I made that one!" Becca pointed at the sparkle and streamers of SAVE THIS TREE.

Julie directed everybody out to the sidewalk to sign the petition Dad held on a clipboard. He stood by another big sign they'd made last night, TREE SIT-IN. It was nailed to a stake, and that morning on his way to work Dad had pounded it into the ground near the sidewalk, in Gracie's front yard.

Sandy claimed the right to climb first to the top of the tree, "to show it I can." Then Barry and Arnold took command of the tower room, where they whooped it up, yelling, "Hey, everybody! Help save the tree!"

Saying, "This is the best place to face the cameras," Sandy settled on the front-porch bough and posted Tanya on the staircase. "Julie, this is more fun than the circus!"

"Yeah!" First she needed to find out what had happened when Miss Fogarty had talked to Frank Bailey. Julie hurried through the alley, feeling hot with excitement and embarrassment. She wasn't used to running with a pack of kids, and never had she gotten them into action on something she'd thought up herself.

The little woman wasn't in the back yard. As Julie went to the back door, Squirrel screamed at her from the pear tree, where he had fled when the first wave of children hit the mulberry tree. Miss Fogarty didn't answer the door. She wouldn't desert them at a time like this. Maybe she had gone to bring the city people to the sit-in!

When Julie got back, she saw Dad showing the petition to an elderly man with a cane. He signed the paper, and two people came out of the factory, Chester and who? It was Mr. Potter, the owner. They both signed the petition. Wow!

Sandy was chanting, "Hey! Hey!" with the boys,

and Ned came down the path—"Leave me a place!"—ushering Shelley and Bonnie and their doll strollers. They unpacked their dolls and animals and spread them on the ground below Sandy's swinging legs.

"They all fell out of the tree," Shelley said, flinging doll legs and arms in positions of distress.

"They're all dead," Bonnie said, turning animals on their backs with their legs up.

"Ned," Julie took him aside, "Miss Fogarty is gone again. Maybe she went to get the city people."

"Let's hope! It's—this—" His eyes glistened green at her. "It's going to work, isn't it? The tree sit-in?"

"It's working, the sit-in is happening. Whether it saves the tree—" She raised her shoulders and held them there, looking at him. "So where do you want to be?"

"Guess I'll do some gymnastics for the photographer." He climbed to the elbow-branch and swung by his knees.

Julie stepped around him, scrootched by Tanya on the staircase and climbed up past Becca, who had cozied into the living room branches. Nearby she had hung another beautiful sign she'd made: SQUIRREL'S HAPPY HOME.

"Julie, this is the most fun of anything!" Becca exclaimed. "And don't you worry, it'll do some good."

"It better!" Julie edged out to her place in the side attic and looked around at all the kids. They made so much chatter in the tree, she barely heard the factory going *ti-clack*. There was a person in each room of the Armstrong Apartments.

"So, hey, Julie!" Sandy called up through the tree. "Now we're all ready. Where's the photographer?"

"Be here soon, I hope."

It wasn't a big hope. When she'd phoned the newspaper today, the young man only said he might come, if he got time.

As cars passed, Julie saw heads turn to look at the Sit-In sign and then glance toward the commotion in the tree. Some cars slowed up, and then one stopped. Becca's mother got out. She had a camera, and other cars stopped while she stood in the street to take a picture of the sign and the whole scene.

Coming closer to the tree, she said, "Hey, everybody, listen. I'm going to take pictures of you cute kiddies, so smile and wave."

They did, and Julie did, feeling foolish. Cute kiddies! She saw a man taking pictures, too, with a professional-looking camera. The newspaper photographer? Chester came hustling out of the factory again toward the sit-in.

Grinning, he said, "Let me get in a picture." He chinned himself on Sandy's branch, gulping, "Now! Now! You got it?"

Sandy called to the photographer, "Are you from the newspaper?"

"Yes. Now who started this? What's the story?"

Becca's mother began talking to him.

123

Then Julie saw Miss Fogarty trotting along the sidewalk in a trim little black pantsuit. There was no one with her.

"Miss Fogarty!" Julie called, but her voice was lost in the noise of the boys at the top calling, "Hey! Hey!"

Miss Fogarty marched to the foot of the tree. "All right, all of you, listen!" she commanded. "You can get down now. This is what!"

10

"What's what? Who's she?" Barry and Arnold shouted, not moving from the top of the tree.

"Maybe we've won!" Julie called. "Come on!" She climbed down, urging Becca and Tanya ahead of her.

"Have we saved the tree?" Sandy asked. She dropped from the low bough, landing on a doll so hard the stuffing oozed. Bonnie wailed, and Chester laughed.

Ned swung off his trapeze bough and ran to Miss Fogarty, who stood among the strewn dolls and animals. "Did you make them give up?"

"Yes and no. They'll leave the tree and—"

"Yay!" yelled Arnold and Barry, hurrying down the tree.

"Hush that hollering and listen! The city will leave the tree on a twenty-foot strip of land. But only if somebody buys it. Who's got five hundred dollars?" Her mouth went into a straight line.

Ned and some others shuffled, saying, "But we can't— What do you mean?"

Julie clenched her hands, waiting to hear it.

"I've been back and forth with them all day." Miss Fogarty said she'd talked with Frank Bailey and the City Manager, and they'd talked with members of the City Council. Hearing of the opposition, "Especially mine!" to cutting down the tree, they had agreed to a slightly smaller parking lot.

However, that meant fewer parking meters and less money taken in from them over the years. They said the city could not afford to donate the tree's piece of land and take care of another park. But they would sell it to make up the lost meter money.

"And they'll collect a little in property taxes every year from an owner," she said. "Five hundred dollars isn't much, but I haven't got a penny to spare. Has anybody?" She glanced at Becca's mother and Julie's father.

Julie looked down, to not see Dad's sorry face. She knew he didn't have any money to spare, either.

"Maybe we could get the money somehow," she said. "How long will they wait?"

Ned said, "Yeah, we could have bake sales."

"And ask for donations," Sandy said.

"They have to know by day after tomorrow," Miss Fogarty said.

Some of the kids shrugged and shook their heads. The newspaper photographer walked away.

"Well, kiddies, it was a nice try, and I'm proud of you," said Becca's mother. "We'd better go, honey."

Everyone began to leave. Arnold told Julie maybe he'd think of something, but he was just being nice.

"Well, that's it." Miss Fogarty started toward her house. Julie called after her, "Thank you. Thank you for all your trying." Then she went home with Dad.

In the tower room of her enchanted castle Julie looked out her bedroom window to see magical things. Maybe that was a fairy flying below a cloud—maybe a fairy godmother bringing a sack of gold. She shook her head at herself.

If she wanted to make daydreams, she might as well imagine Dad buying the land and building a house for them where Gracie's house had been.

It couldn't happen. Dad had a hard enough time paying Frannie the money she'd loaned for his college tuition. Money! It was hateful to think only money would keep the tree alive.

Julie slumped on her bed, but the tears didn't come. She kept thinking, *It's a chance.* The city people had given her a chance to save the tree. It looked impossible and yet— She punched her pillow up and leaned against it. Where could she get the money to buy the tree?

She couldn't ask her grandmother, because they already owed her money and Gram wasn't rich. How could she earn some money? Baby-sitting, delivering newspapers . . . not enough. She needed a real job, like Chester had.

Julie sat up. The factory! Maybe she could get a job at Potter's factory. But Mr. Potter might think she was only a child— She brushed that aside. Surely there was something she could do. After school, Saturdays . . . If the city would let her pay some down on the land and so much a week . . .

What time was it? Twenty till six. Chester left the factory around five o'clock. Maybe the place would be closed by now.

Julie ran downstairs and called to Dad in the kitchen, "I've got an idea! Gotta hurry. Be back soon."

As she raced down the sidewalk, she saw a short man come out of the factory in the next block and start to walk away.

"Mr. Potter! Wait!" she yelled.

Oh, what a bad beginning! But the figure turned and waited.

When she puffed up to him, Mr. Potter said,

"What? Oh, you're the girl who— Say, Chester told me what happened. Said the only way to save the tree is to buy the land."

"That's what"—she gasped for breath—"I want to talk to you about. I'm going to buy it."

Smile creases appeared on his round face. "Yes?"

The factory was silent, no clacking. All the workers seemed to have left. How could she ask a near stranger for a job? Julie took a deep breath so she could talk evenly.

"I need to earn money to buy the tree. Five hundred dollars. Sir, can I work at your factory? After school and Saturdays. I'll do anything."

He put his hands in his pockets. "Well now, do you have any experience with machines?"

He was making a joke of it. Once she'd seen a woman sitting at a machine.

"No, but I could learn. And I could—um—print labels on boxes, run errands, and I can sweep as well as Chester. I'm good at washing windows." She pointed to the row of big dirty windows with two stories of wide windows above them.

"Hm, they do need washing—always do." He jingled coins in a pocket. "Well, I wonder." He looked in at his machines. "Child labor laws wouldn't allow you in there. Still, maybe you could run some errands for me—I'd have to check. But . . . a child . . . you'd get tired of the work."

"I wouldn't!"

He looked at her again, and she realized she'd clasped her hands, as if she were praying.

"Well . . . what's your name—Julie? I've seen you stick to that tree. Maybe you'd stick to this. I'd like to help you. I could try to give you work after school, half days on Saturdays, three dollars and a quarter an hour."

"Oh, Mr. Potter!"

"But that might not solve the problem. Do you realize how long you'd have to work to earn five hundred dollars? And what if, after all your work, the tree fell over in a storm someday?"

They both looked across at the tree, still waving its banners. DON'T KILL ME, she read her sign.

"Ye-es, but it's lasted a hundred years of storms," Julie said. "If the tree went that way, it would be natural, not chopped down."

"Been there all my life," he mused. "I'm used to seeing it." He turned to her. "However, the problem is, I don't think the city will wait for you to earn five hundred dollars."

"I've got fifteen dollars saved," she began, but he talked on.

"I've been thinking about the land, anyway, since you staged that sit-in. Some show! Like to keep some greenery in the neighborhood. See, I had trees planted last spring. Pin oaks."

He pointed to a line of sticks in the ground between the sidewalk and the street. Even though each one had a few leaves on it, Julie hadn't even thought of them as trees. Poor spindly things no taller than she was.

"That could be part of your job," the man told her. "Keep them watered and find out from the nursery what they need to protect them through the winter."

She nodded. "Sure, I could. But if the city people won't wait for the money—"

"This is what I can do. I'll pay the city their five hundred dollars, and you can work off half the cost. That would save me half of the outlay of money," Mr. Potter said to her seriously, "so don't leave me stuck with it. When you've worked off two hundred and fifty dollars, your name goes on the deed as half owner of the land. Would you agree to that?"

It was so strange to stand here on the sidewalk talking business with a man she hardly knew. His idea meant she'd be only half owner of the tree. But that didn't matter. She'd never really wanted to *own* it, she realized, any more than she'd think of owning Squirrel.

"Partners?" He smiled.

"Oh, yes! Oh, thank you! But—"

She remembered about the property taxes, and he said those wouldn't amount to more than twenty dollars on such a small lot of unimproved land. Next year, when taxes came due, they could work that out. Meantime, she could come in after school tomorrow and start washing windows on the outside.

"All right! I'll be here as soon as I get off the school bus!"

He laughed, walking away to where his car was parked. "You sound like a go-getter," he called back.

The air seemed to swell in Julie's chest. She waited a moment, then ran across the street.

"Tree, you're safe!" She thumped the trunk. "You're safe!" She ran through the alley to Miss Fogarty's back door.

The woman answered her knock, looking gloomy. "I'm having some chicken noodle soup to comfort me. Want some?"

"No—no, thank you— Oh, Miss Fogarty! The tree is safe! I'm going to buy it!"

"Come in." Sharply she said, "Grandma going to give you the money?"

"No! I'm going to earn it. I've got a job!"

Julie sat at the kitchen table, while Miss Fogarty ate her soup, and told all about it. "And I start work tomorrow!"

"So Potter's going to pay for the land. Do tell! And you— If you're working all the time, I guess I won't see you up in that tree much."

She didn't sound as happy as Julie had expected. "You will. I'll go there Sundays and— Aren't you glad at all?"

Miss Fogarty shoved her bowl aside. "Of course I'm glad!" Some of the wrinkles in her tough-nut face were smile lines. "I'm glad the tree is safe. Mostly I'm glad for you. I don't have to be glad to live next door to a public park."

"Maybe it won't be any more public than it was before. Maybe Mr. Potter will agree to leave the land just as it is, except," Julie guessed, "maybe a picnic table. For his workers to eat lunch in good weather."

Miss Fogarty glanced out the window. "I wonder how soon it will snow. Potter Park!"

Sometimes Miss Fogarty's grumpiness was funny. Laughing, Julie said, "I'll have half rights to name it. Let's name it," she coaxed, "Mulberry Park. No, Mabel Mulberry Park!"

"Hah!" Miss Fogarty gave her dry chuckle at last. "All right."

"Now I have to go tell Dad. And call Ned. Oh boy!" Julie whirled away again.

Early the next morning, before school-bus time, Julie went to the tree. For the first time in days she could climb it without fearing it would be destroyed. Dear Mabel Mulberry . . . River Queen . . . Armstrong Apartments.

As she mounted into the crotch, Squirrel scampered out on a branch and chattered at her.

"You're safe, Squirrel. Your home is safe!"

Posters and signs still fluttered from boughs in the breeze. After school Ned was going to take them down and maybe get some of the kids to help. When she'd phoned him last night, he'd been so excited he'd come down to her house to hear all about it.

"You really are the best girl I know!" Ned declared. Then to cover any mushiness, he'd teased, "I'll wave to you from the tree while you work."

Julie leaned against a living-room branch. It was going to be fun to tell Becca and Sandy and the others the wonderful news. She'd make sure she got to the bus stop first, before Ned told! If they came after school to help Ned, she'd see them up here in the tree, while she washed windows. Maybe she'd see them in the tree other times, when she was working.

She let out a little sigh. She'd have to get used to that. But it was all right. Really, everything was all right! Wait till Frannie found out about this! She approved of work. By the time she came next weekend, Julie wanted to have those factory windows fairly sparkling.

She climbed on up to the tower room in time to see her father going into the factory. After he'd gotten used to the idea of her working—"A job! Now wait a minute!"—he'd had doubts about her being around dangerous machinery. "At least let me talk to Mr. Potter and take a look at the place." Julie wasn't worried. She didn't think Mr. Potter would let her get near his precious greasy machines.

The rising sun warmed her head. Just this

once . . . Julie edged up one branch higher than she'd dared go before.

That was the thing about climbing a tree: She always wanted to go higher, as if there should be more above. What if she could walk in giant steps from one green mound of tree to another? Or like Jack, climbing the beanstalk, she might step out into another world!

Julie had the dizzy feeling she was about to discover something important. But the vision flickered away.

She let herself down to her usual perch. Sitting in the tower, she looked out over the beautiful world of Sutterville. By Sunday she might be sitting up here and looking down on what the bulldozers had done to Wilder-land. Yet it still would be a beautiful world, because she'd be seeing it from the top of this tree.